# The GOLDEN ROSE

*Dayle Campbell Gaetz*

Pacific Educational Press
Vancouver Canada

Published by Pacific Educational Press
Faculty of Education
University of British Columbia
Vancouver, B.C.
V6T 1Z4
Telephone (604) 822-5385
Fax (604) 822-6603

The publisher would like to thank Canadian Heritage, the
Canada Council, and the Province of British Columbia for
their financial assistance. In addition, the publisher would
like to thank Sarah Heslop for acting as a model for the
cover illustration.

**Canadian Cataloguing in Publication**
Gaetz, Dayle, 1947-
  The golden rose

  ISBN 1-895766-21-4

  1. Frontier and pioneer life--British Columbia--Hope -Juvenile
fiction. 2. Fraser River Valley (B.C.)--Gold discoveries--
Juvenile fiction. I. Title.
PS8563.A25317G64 1996     jC813'.54     C96-910652-1
PZ7.G1185Go 1996

Cover illustration by Linda Heslop
Edited by Carolyn Sale
Cover design by Warren Clark
Printed in Canada

10 9 8 7 6 5 4 3 2 1

# Contents

# Chapter 1

Katherine pointed into the distance. "Look!" she cried, then glanced quickly about to see if Mother were nearby. Her mother would frown and remind her that it was rude to point. Or was it only rude to point at people? Right now Katherine was too excited to care.

She touched Susan's arm and pointed again, at a tiny speck on the horizon. "Land!" she said, and her whole body tingled with excitement. The speck grew, took on colour, became a small island. More islands pushed themselves up out of the sea as the steamer approached. Weak, shrivelled people with pale faces appeared on deck and milled about, blinking in the brilliant sunshine like moles emerging from their holes.

Katherine had spent ten days on this ship, but not one face looked even vaguely familiar. She watched Susan move among the people on deck, stopping often to speak, smiling, exchanging greetings as if these people were old friends. Suddenly Katherine turned cold, in spite of the hot sun: for the first time she noticed how much her sister had changed. Susan's sky blue eyes no longer sparkled and her lovely hair — the warm, mellow colour of gold — had lost its shine. Her oval face, usually glowing with health, had become pale, almost grey. Susan looked years older than she had when they pulled away from Southampton only ten days ago. But she's still beautiful, Katherine realized with a stab of envy — even now. She turned away and stared down at the waves lapping against the side of the steamer.

Katherine had always shrunk from being compared with her sister. She herself was too thin — bony, some of the boys called her at home. Her face was long, narrow, and far too pale, even when she was feeling well; her nose was a little too pointed and her eyes just slightly too small. She was not smart like Susan either, and did not have one-tenth of her sister's self-confidence. To top it all off, since leaving England, Katherine had discovered that Susan was immune to seasickness. She closed her eyes and silently prayed, as she had so many times lately, that she would discover something, some one thing, she could do better than Susan. "And," she whispered, "if it's not too much trouble, could it possibly happen by my fourteenth birthday?"

A shudder went through the ship as the engine sound changed. Katherine opened her eyes. Another, smaller steamer was approaching. The two ships pulled alongside one another and many of the passengers began to transfer from the larger vessel to the smaller one.

Katherine was amazed when a young, well-dressed woman holding a small child in one arm threw her free arm around Susan. There were tears in the mother's eyes as she turned away. Who was she? How did Susan know her? The woman's husband shook Susan's hand and said something before hurrying after his small family. For a moment Susan stood quietly, looking down at the palm of her hand, then she called after the couple, waving her arm in the air, "No, I shouldn't have this!" but it was too late; they were gone.

"What's that?" Katherine asked, walking over.

"A gold nugget — apparently a most unusual one." Susan held it up. "See? It looks just like a rose, as if someone had carved it that way." She slid it into her pocket and shuddered, just as the ship had. "You know I've never liked roses. I only hope . . ."

"But — who were those people?" Katherine interrupted.

"Oh, Mr. and Mrs. Roberts. They're returning to their plantation in Jamaica after a vacation in England. I can't believe they think I saved their baby's life! I didn't really, I just took care of her when everyone was sick."

"That's why they gave you the nugget?"

Susan nodded. "They said it was a charm, that it will bring me luck in our new home, because that's where it came from. Mr. Roberts' brother owns a store in some little British Columbia town — now, what was it called? Yale, I think. Anyway, this brother sent the nugget to them after their baby was born. He thought it was fitting because her name is Rose."

When the ship started up once more, Katherine remained on deck to watch it steam into a horseshoe-shaped harbour in a small, hilly island known as St. Thomas. Here the family moved onto a much smaller ship.

The sun beat down from high overhead and the winds dropped to almost nothing as they were whisked across the Caribbean Sea. Someone joined Katherine on deck. She glanced up in surprise. She had not seen her brother for days, even though Susan told her he had not been seasick. He stood with his feet planted wide apart and his arms folded across his chest. The warm breeze whipped his light brown curls about his face and his arrogant blue eyes squinted against the bright sun. "I can hardly wait to reach dry land and leave this bloody ship behind," he grumbled.

Katherine assumed he was speaking to her, but only because no one else was within hearing. "Yes," she agreed, "it has been a horrid voyage."

"Boring," he said, "I've never been so bored in all my life. And everyone had to get sick so there was no one to talk to."

"Oh, poor George," she said bitterly. "How inconsiderate of us!"

He had rested his elbows against the ship's railing, but

now he stood up and pushed himself away. He glared down at Katherine as if she were a small, foolish child. George had thick, sand-brown eyebrows and dark blue eyes that always seemed cold and distant. His strong, Roman nose, wide, sensitive lips, and bold chin made him, at nineteen, a good-looking young man. At least that's what the girls in England seemed to think. Katherine thought he was stuffy and completely filled with his own importance.

George yawned. "I should have known you wouldn't understand. For an intelligent person to be cooped up day after day with nothing to do is the worst kind of torture."

Katherine thought of the terrible seasickness she had endured, unable to eat, her head pounding with unimaginable pain. If it had not been for Susan who visited her every day, helped her out onto deck, and brought her cups of broth that she was barely able to sip, Katherine was not at all certain she would have survived. She knew Susan had also been nursing their parents — as well as, it seemed, many others on board. "You could have helped Susan," she retorted, mainly because she could think of nothing else to say.

George peered over his nose at her. He opened his mouth as if to speak but then thought better of it. He shook his head very slightly, and pulled his eyebrows together in a gesture calculated to make her feel small and insignificant, then he turned and sauntered away.

The steamer chugged slowly through the marshy waters of Limón Bay and landed at a brand-new town, built up from swamp-wet earth and rocks that had been carried out through the jungle as the railroad line was pushed through. Colón existed only because of the five-year-old railroad constructed to carry people across the narrow isthmus to the Pacific Ocean. The town provided a stopover, a place where passengers could rest until their train was ready to leave.

As soon as the boat docked, Katherine rushed ahead of

her family with one thing on her mind. Land. Solid, dry land. Land that did not move beneath her feet. She had not gone far before she stopped as abruptly as if she had slammed into a wall. Like a sudden fever, the tropical heat flowed over her, from her ankles to the roots of her hair. Then the ground began to sway, very slightly, this way and that. Her stomach rolled into a tight, hard knot. She turned dizzily, trying to see her family, but the bright scene before her faded to dark, brightened, then faded again. Somewhere, perhaps inside her own head, a shrill bell started ringing. It blotted out all other sounds. She took one shaky step before everything went black.

Gradually she became aware of a voice calling her name and hands gripping her shoulders, shaking her. She tried to push the hands away but they held on too tightly; she tried to say, "Go away, leave me alone," but her voice refused to work. She forced her eyes open.

Through the dazzling sunlight she managed to focus on her sister's face: a gaunt, pale face with a deep line etched between her thin eyebrows. Susan's eyes were filled with concern and Katherine wondered why. Then she saw Mother looming above her, swaying a little as if she were on the deck of a ship, and Katherine suddenly realized that she was lying, flat out, on a warm and dusty road. In the same instant, she realized something was wrong with her mother.

Before this journey Mother had been a strong, graceful woman, fiercely proud of her narrow waist and youthful good looks, but now her shoulders stooped and her eyes held a look of sad defeat. Seeing her, Katherine felt a sudden sense of loss, an emptiness she could not begin to understand.

Mother tucked a stray wisp of her faded hair behind one ear and looked down at Katherine. "Just see what is happening to us! It's so hot here one can barely breathe!" Her face turned bitter. "We should never have come. I never wanted to leave England." She pressed her fists against her forehead. "If only your father — "

"What's going on here?" Father stormed up, his face bright red and beads of perspiration glistening on his forehead. He was a tall, thin man whose dark hair was getting sparse on top. He had a high, narrow nose and dark eyes that flashed down angrily at Katherine. "Kate, will you get up? This is no time to rest, you'll make us miss the train."

"It so happens that she fainted," Mother told him. "The poor girl is exhausted. She hasn't eaten in a week and she needs water desperately."

"A daughter of mine faint? Impossible! Why, Kate is as strong as an ox. Come along my girl. If we miss that train there's no telling how long we may be stranded in this miserable place." He swung around on his heel and marched away. "Follow me," he called over his shoulder. "Don't let's get lost."

Without a glance at any of them, George followed.

Mother threw up her hands. "Can't you see the girl — "

"I'm all right, Mother." Katherine struggled to her feet with Susan's help. She swayed a little and the ground shifted uneasily beneath her. Her stomach turned over. She swallowed and willed herself to be strong. "If only the ground would stop moving," she murmured. "What's wrong with this place? I feel as if I'm still aboard ship."

"I know," Susan told her, "but it isn't really moving at all. They say it takes a few days to adjust to being on solid ground. And by then . . . "

Katherine and Mother exchanged glances. They both shuddered. No one voiced the thought in all of their minds. By then they would be at Panama City making ready to board another ship.

"As if the heat weren't bad enough, we have to be plagued by insects as well." Mother slapped her husband across the ear. "There's one that will not live to bite again!" She almost smiled, but quickly clapped her handkerchief over her mouth and nose. "You mustn't breathe the air," she warned her family — for perhaps the sixth time. Katherine had lost count. "The vapours from the swamp carry fever, you know."

The little train rattled along its track, a narrow slice cut through dense, tropical jungle. Heat rose from the very floor-boards, carrying with it mingled smells of metal, smoke, and decay. Katherine's nostrils were dry and clogged with dust. She could not get enough air into her lungs, especially with the foolish handkerchief over her face. Whenever Mother looked away, she removed it and breathed as deeply as she could.

Hot and mosquito-ridden as it was, the train was better by far than the ship. Her stomach was calm, not the least bit woozy. She felt light and free, as she imagined a prisoner must feel upon being released.

"They say that for every single tie put down, a man died in building this railroad," Father informed them. "Work-ers were imported by the thousands from China and Eu-rope. When most of them took sick and died of panama fe-ver, more were brought in to replace them. It took almost five years and eight million dollars to build only forty-five miles of track. It is the most expensive railroad ever built."

Something caught Katherine's eye and she turned to look out the window. Brilliant greens and muted greys flashed against the lush green leaves of the tropical forest. Katherine leaned her cheek against the dusty window to watch parrots fly from branch to branch high above the tracks. Watching them, she forgot all about the heat and the mosquitoes.

Suddenly she sat up straighter and pressed her nose to the window. Perched on a branch and blinking down at her was a tiny monkey. It dropped down and hung by one long, hairy arm then reached out with its other arm and swung with ease to a second branch. The little human-like forms were everywhere then, swinging along in the same direc-tion as the train and watching the people inside as curiously as the people watched them. Tiny babies clung precariously to their mothers' chests as they swung through the treetops. Katherine envied them up there in the cool, green canopy, able to munch on succulent leaves when they pleased, not encumbered by heavy skirts and petticoats that stuck to your legs and held the heat against your body.

"Would you rather be a parrot or a monkey?" she asked Susan.

When Susan did not answer Katherine turned to look at her older sister. Susan's eyes were closed. Her long, fair lashes shaded the dark circles under her eyes, making them appear even darker. Something inside Katherine twisted in alarm. Her sister looked so frail. And why didn't she answer? Katherine reached over, grabbed Susan's arm, and shook her. The lashes fluttered and her eyes opened, red-rimmed, the blue no longer blue at all but faded to a tired grey. Susan's eyes darted about as if she had forgotten where she was. Then they settled on Katherine, curious. If she were annoyed she did not let it show.

"Would you rather be a parrot or a monkey?" Katherine repeated.

Susan frowned slightly and looked out the window. Gradually a smile turned up the corners of her mouth. "A monkey," she said eagerly. "It would be such fun to swing through the branches and sit in the shade laughing at the foolish people down below in their hot and dusty little train."

Katherine laughed aloud, she was so relieved to hear her sister talking like her old self. "As for me, I'd rather be a parrot. I would fly wherever I wanted to go and no one could tell me what to do ever again."

They watched for a long while, fascinated. The train crossed a narrow bridge over a lazy, mud-brown river. "Look at that!" Katherine's voice cracked with the dryness and dust; her tongue felt as if it had swollen and become glued to the roof of her mouth. "A giant mud pie!" she rasped. But Susan did not answer. She had fallen asleep once more.

"Look, children," Father announced, "this is the Chagres River." His long nose lifted and sniffed the air. "The water is not especially clean. Did I mention this railroad is important for carrying mining equipment to California and hauling the gold back to New York? George, listen to this . . . "

A smell rose up from the river, a smell that turned her stomach. Katherine wrinkled her nose. She settled back, shutting her ears to the drone of mosquitoes and her father's voice. Soon she fell asleep and dreamed that she and Susan walked beside a cool stream trickling through a quiet meadow.

The five of them stood outside their hotel in Panama City, gazing up in wonder. An old Spanish palace with tall marble pillars, it had been built more than two hundred years earlier when the Spanish were the only Europeans on the west coast of America. After travelling so far across rough seas and through uninhabited jungle, the Harrises had finally arrived at an oasis of civilization. It seemed too good to be real. Katherine squeezed her eyes shut and opened them again. The hotel was still there. Its thick walls assured her the air would be cooler inside. And surely there would be a bathtub. They hurried through the high, arched doorway and stopped again, astonished at the grand stairway curving gracefully toward the floor above.

Inside, the air was noticeably cooler. "Oh, no!" cried Susan looking up toward the high ceiling where large punkahs slowly turned, moving the stale, warm air. It took Katherine a minute to realize that the huge, black clouds drifting beneath the fans were seething, whining clusters of mosquitoes waiting impatiently for a taste of human flesh.

As soon as they reached their room, Katherine ran toward the bathtub, a large oval of cool marble just waiting to soak away the dust and grime and stickiness of travel. It was magnificent. She could hardly wait to climb into it.

Her excitement did not last long. The water turned out to be a sickening brownish-yellow that smelled disgusting. Katherine dropped to her knees in dismay. It must have come directly from that muddy river they had passed.

There was a soft groan behind her and Katherine turned to look up at her sister's face. A tear spilled out of each eye and trickled in tiny rivulets through the brown dust of her cheeks.

Alarmed, Katherine jumped up and threw her arms around Susan. Her sister never cried. Susan was the strong one, always holding everyone together. A little twinge of fear pulled at Katherine's stomach.

"Never mind, Suz," she said, "we can wash off at least. We'll get rid of this awful dust and put on clean frocks. Then we'll feel better, you'll see. After that we'll have a nice dinner in the dining room and drink gallons of water. Everything will be all right, really it will."

Susan nibbled at her lower lip and blinked her eyes, trying to stop the tears. She wiped at them and her face became a muddy mask.

Katherine could not stop talking. She had to cheer Susan up. Seeing her sister like this gave her a nervous, jittery feeling slightly below her ribcage. "And soon we'll be in Victoria." Katherine winced and pushed away the thought of another sea voyage. "I'm sure they'll have lots of water in Victoria. So much water you can have a bath every day — two if you want. And it will be clean. So clean and clear you can hardly see it. It will be cool and soft against your skin and . . . and there won't be any mosquitoes."

Saying this, Katherine reached out and slapped a mosquito on Susan's forehead. She looked at the squashed insect, saw how its blood mingled with the dust on her sister's damp brow. She studied the smudges of dust and tears on Susan's cheeks, and, without knowing she was going to, started laughing. She laughed and tried to stop and laughed even harder. The laughter bubbled up from deep inside and overflowed, out of control.

Susan gave her a stern look and Katherine could only point at her sister helplessly, and nod at a mirror and the disgusting brown water beginning to congeal in the bath-tub. She shook her head helplessly. With her two index fingers she drew circles around her own eyes in the dust she knew must be there and traced lines from her nose to the edges of her mouth. Susan looked in the mirror. She stared at Katherine. And then she burst out laughing, as helplessly as her younger sister.

The rest of the family gathered around with curious faces that reminded Katherine of the monkeys they had seen. And this made her laugh even harder. The two girls could only point at one another, at the dust, the red blotch that had been a mosquito, at Katherine's clownish face and the brown, smelly water lying in the tub with mosquitoes already hovering over it. Mother shook her head sadly. George guffawed once and glanced at Father who stared grimly at the two girls and crossed his arms over his chest. George swallowed and copied him.

How could Katherine explain what was so funny? Nothing was, really. Only the fact that everything was so desperately, disappointingly horrible.

When the laughter subsided, Katherine was thirstier than ever. So thirsty she no longer cared how dirty the water was, she would drink it. She lifted a glass to her mouth.

"You'll catch your death!" Her mother, horrified, snatched away the glass of smelly brown water before Katherine got so much as a taste.

"But I'm already dying of thirst!" she whined. Her tongue stuck against the roof of her mouth, her throat felt like dry sawdust.

"You'll die of something a thousand times worse than thirst if you drink this disgusting water." Mother stared into the glass and her bottom lip quivered. "Oh, how I wish we'd never left England. I never wanted to, you know, your father . . . "

"If I'm going to die anyway, why not die in comfort?"

Her mother glared through narrowed eyes, her face a paler, thinner, older version of Susan's. "My dear girl, have you never heard of dysentery?"

Katherine nodded. She had heard of it, of course. She knew dysentery was a disease people feared, but she could not imagine it would be worse than this horrible, burning thirst.

Her mother leaned closer and whispered, "Terrifying cramps, endless diarrhea, raging fever."

Katherine shrugged, unimpressed.

"It's a thousand times worse than being seasick."

"Oh!" Katherine groaned. She eyed the brown water with a strange kind of respect.

The hotel dining room was elaborate, with high ceilings, marble columns, and arched doorways. Even Mother seemed impressed. The waiter filled her glass with wine, then moved on to Father's and George's. When he stopped beside Susan, Mother objected.

"I'm afraid we don't allow young ladies to consume wine in England," she said. "It isn't good for them. It affects their behaviour, you know."

"Si, Senora," he said and proceeded to fill up the glass.

"Hmmph," said Mother, so loudly other diners turned to look. The waiter moved on to Katherine. "As for children," she added, "they are never served wine in England. It would be simply too outrageous."

The waiter nodded and leaned over Katherine's wine glass.

"Do I not make myself clear?" Mother spoke very slowly as if that and the loudness of her voice could somehow make him understand a language he did not know. "In England we do not give alcoholic beverages to children."

The waiter looked at her and frowned slightly. Then he

nodded politely and filled Katherine's glass. Katherine reached for the cool glass of liquid, took a big gulp, gasped and plunked it down again. Her throat was on fire; tears streamed down her face.

"There, you see what you have done?" Mother glared at the waiter.

"I'll handle this," said Father, leaning forward in his chair. "Agua, por el leettle one, Senor waiter, por favor."

"I'm not *leettle*," Katherine objected. "I'm thirteen years old and I'm tired of being treated as if I was a child."

"As if I were . . . " corrected Mother.

The waiter smiled calmly. "Agua is not fit to drink," he said.

"But — " Father's jaw dropped.

Mother drew herself up angrily and squared her shoulders. "We assumed you could not understand English."

"Si? But I have studied the English."

"Then why on earth did you give wine to the child when I specifically asked you not to?"

His eyes widened in surprise. "But you do not ask me this. You only explain that children and young ladies in England do not drink the wine."

Mrs. Harris smiled in triumph. "Precisely," she said. "So, may I ask why you gave wine to my children?"

"But, Senora, this is not England, this is Panama!"

Katherine thought she heard a chuckle from George but when she glanced at him he was quietly sipping his wine and staring fixedly at something on the far side of the dining room.

"Well! I never — "

"He does have a point there," said Father. "This is Panama, not England, and if the water is unfit to drink we mustn't let our girls go thirsty. Especially in this heat. Besides, I've heard that alcohol helps ward off the effects of the fever."

He raised his glass and took a long drink.

Katherine bit her lip and covered her mouth as if suppressing a cough. She did not dare look at Susan.

# Chapter 2

Katherine stood on the wharf looking down at the waves that gently lapped against the pilings beneath her feet. The Pacific Ocean. She now stood on the opposite side of the world from the Atlantic and home. Would she ever see England again? Her heart felt heavy, remembering her grandmother standing alone on the dock at Southampton, fighting back tears. For the first time Katherine had a sense of how her mother must feel. She had been forced, against her will, to leave behind not only her friends and family but her very idea of civilization.

Katherine wished her mother could understand the excitement she and Susan shared. Wild and free, that's how they saw their new country and their new lives. Katherine ignored the flutter of fear that she felt whenever she thought about the wilderness awaiting them. She was certain Susan never felt any such misgivings.

Voices began to penetrate Katherine's thoughts and she realized Father had struck up a conversation. She turned her head slightly, just enough to observe, out of the corner of her eye, a plump gentleman wearing a wide-brimmed hat. As long as she did not look directly at them, she knew they would talk as if she were not present. Adults were like that, they assumed children needed both their eyes and their ears in order to hear. Katherine had no objection to taking advantage of that fact.

"Yes," the gentleman nodded, "I'm perfectly satisfied. Two summers and one dreadful winter on my claim and I have enough to retire very comfortably. I'm on my way home to England now. I've had enough of wilderness and living like a savage to last me the rest of my life."

"So you believe it's still possible to make your fortune in gold?" She could not quite see her father and did not dare turn her head further, but she recognized the unconcealed excitement in his voice.

The man nodded. "With the Fraser wiped clean, they're heading north by the thousands. The Cariboo is the richest yet, you mark my words."

"I'm taking my family to Victoria," Father explained.

"Victoria, you say? Then I hope you have been vaccinated against the smallpox. Last I heard the town was in the midst of an epidemic."

"We most likely will not stay long in Victoria. I plan to purchase some land, then perhaps do a little mining."

Katherine was so surprised she almost jerked her head around to study his face and determine if he were serious. Mining? What had happened to farming? Not that any of them knew anything about farming, but at least they might be able to grow enough food to keep from starving. You could not eat gold. She wondered if her mother knew about this mining idea.

"Ah," said the man, "then Hope is the place you want to settle. Busy little town, head of navigation, end of the Brigade Trail. It will be the start of the new road to the Cariboo before long, too, if I'm not mistaken. Great future in Hope."

"Indeed. I'll certainly look into that when we get to Victoria."

"Say, you're not thinking of taking the *John L. Stephens*?"

"Why, yes." Father sounded somewhat annoyed. "We board in four days."

The man stepped closer to Father, out of Katherine's

line of sight. In a hoarse, easily overheard whisper, he said, "Of course you know what they call that ship?"

"Of course," said Father and Katherine smiled because she knew he had no idea. She turned her head slightly, just enough to see the man again.

"Right." The plump man tucked his thumbs into his belt and rolled back on his heels. "The floating coffin."

The smile vanished from Katherine's face. She glanced around to see if any of the others had heard. But her mother and Susan were standing at the edge of the wharf watching men load heavy, iron objects onto a ship. Then she spotted George. He stood with his back to her. His hands were on his hips and his head half turned as if he too were listening.

"Yes," Father chuckled nervously, "but have you any idea why?"

"Indeed! That old ship is a death-trap! It's always over-crowded with men racing for the gold fields and it's most unseaworthy. It will sink straight to the bottom one day soon, you mark my words."

"Remember this moment," said Father when the family assembled on the deck of the *John L. Stephens*. "This is our first venture onto the Pacific Ocean."

"And perhaps our last," Katherine muttered.

The sun was shining and the sea sparkled with a light chop as they watched Panama disappear behind them. "Imagine crossing from the Atlantic to the Pacific in less than a day," Father mused. "Do you realize how long the Spaniards took to travel that distance in their sailing ships? Going all the way around the tip of South America? Do you know how long it took the fur traders to get from England to Vancouver Island?" His dark eyebrows lowered and he glared at George who was busy studying his feet.

After an uncomfortable silence Susan spoke up. "About six months, wasn't it, George?"

Father's dark eyes flicked to Susan. "Quite right," he muttered. His eyes narrowed and rolled back to George. "And how long will it take us?"

George's eyes rested upon the horizon. The muscles of his face were pulled tight. "About fifty days," Susan whispered.

Father cleared his throat and glared at George. "You must learn to speak up, George, my boy. It doesn't do to let a mere girl answer for you."

George grunted.

Katherine felt a burst of anger. Why shouldn't Susan answer? She had always been smarter than George. Was she supposed to play stupid just to make George look good? Katherine was about to speak her mind when Susan's light touch on her hand made her stop. Susan shook her head ever so slightly and her eyes begged Katherine to remain quiet.

George shrugged. "At least I know what pacific means."

"Of course."

"Calm and peaceful. So you and the women won't get seasick this time," he said.

Katherine braced herself for Father's reply.

"Of course I won't," he snapped. "It's simply a matter of self-control."

No one dared remind him he had been the only one to stay below decks, moaning and complaining for the entire voyage across the Atlantic.

"And before you know it we'll be in San Francisco," he added, clearing his throat to launch into its history.

"Hmmph," Mother put in quickly. "I hope they know better than to give wine to children in that city."

Sometime in the middle of the night Katherine awoke to the sound of creaking timbers. She had the eerie sense that the ship was being lifted into the air and she held her breath as it hung there for an endless moment. Suddenly it plunged straight down, leaving her, or at least her stomach, hanging in the air. Her eyes flew open and she sat up, unable to see a thing in the blackness around her. She wished she had not eaten quite so much dinner. A few minutes later, groping for the bucket Susan had so thoughtfully placed beside her bunk, she wished she had not eaten anything at all.

By the time the steamer, still in one piece, chugged into the harbour at San Francisco, all of them, with the exception of Father, had come down with a disease the ship's captain diagnosed as panama fever. "Not many travel across the isthmus without picking up the fever," he told them. "It's in the air that rises off the swamps. I hear tell they brought in a thousand Chinese workers back in '53. In less than two months they were down to two hundred. The only good part of it is," he went on, "that if you get the fever once and survive, you won't likely get it again."

"We must find a doctor," insisted Mother as soon as they were settled in rooms at a San Francisco hotel.

"No need for a doctor, " Father told her, "I can tell you exactly what the problem is. Simply the change of diet, strange water, and the motion of the ship. You will all be fine in the morning."

The next morning Father also was feverish and vomiting.

"Panama fever," the doctor confirmed and insisted none of them would be fit to travel for at least ten days.

"I just knew this would happen," Mother said sharply. "We've come all this way from home simply to die in a strange, barbaric country."

They did not die, however, and within two weeks had boarded their fourth steamer and made their way up the coast to Vancouver Island. The sea was flat and calm and the sun shone with a comforting warmth as they entered Victoria Harbour. At long last their journey was almost over and Katherine stood on deck, gazing in wonder at everything she saw.

The harbour was dotted with sailing ships and the occasional steamer resting at anchor. Native people in heavy dugout canoes paddled back and forth attending to their own business. Wood and brick buildings clustered along the shoreline, and from there the land sloped gently upward, graced by the tall, rounded shapes of oaks and maples. Standing on the horizon in the background were the sharper outlines of firs and cedars. A tingle of excitement ran through Katherine. Everything in this new land was so different, so vast and so much more rugged than the quiet, cultivated England that had been her home for close to fourteen years.

After finding rooms in the Colonial Hotel, the family ventured out for a look at the little town. Groups of men dressed in suits and hats stood about on wooden sidewalks, chatting; others drove one-horse carts to and fro, raising clouds of dust as they passed. Katherine saw black people and Chinese mingling with native Indians and Europeans, and heard French, German, and English accents along with harsh Yankee voices. She was fascinated.

They stopped at a section of tall, palisaded wall. "This was part of the original Hudson's Bay Company fort," Father informed them. "The walls are being torn down now because the town has outgrown them since the gold rush began."

"Good riddance!" commented a woman standing beside them. "Those great walls were an eyesore and the narrow gates so difficult for us ladies to negotiate in our skirts."

Katherine looked down at the absurdly wide hooped skirt the woman wore. "Then why don't you wear something more comfortable?" she asked.

"It's the fashion," Mother put in quickly with a slight, embarrassed laugh. "You'll understand when you're older."

Katherine clucked her tongue against the roof of her mouth. She thought it was stupid to wear something that looked ridiculous and was uncomfortable just because someone on the other side of the world decided it was fashionable, and she opened her mouth to say so.

"Are you from England as well?" Susan put in hastily, placing a hand firmly on Katherine's shoulder.

"Why, yes. And I must say I miss it terribly."

Katherine stared at the ground. It was beginning to look as if even here, in this little outpost surrounded by giant trees and misty waters, people were no more free than in London. She sighed. Maybe, just maybe, Hope would be different. She hoped Father would decide to go there. It sounded so exciting and so, well, hopeful.

In the evening Susan went up to the room to lie down while the other four took a stroll. The sun was still high in the sky, keeping the air pleasantly warm as they climbed the gentle slope of Beacon Hill. At the top a cool wind blew off the Strait of Juan de Fuca, and Katherine, shivering, pulled her shawl more tightly around her shoulders. She had lost weight in the past weeks and had trouble keeping warm.

Father soon struck up a conversation with a middle-aged couple.

"In winter Victoria becomes a city of tents," said the thin man who sported a huge, greying beard. "Most of the gold miners move down here before the snows begin up in the mountains. They like the mild winters on the coast and they spend lots of money." He chuckled. "That's the reason I opened a store here — it's the surest way to get rich during a gold rush. I sell everything from boots to pickaxes. Even the Indians come to trade — or they did until the sickness hit them."

"Smallpox?"

The man nodded. "A terrible thing — brought here last March by a gold miner from San Francisco. By the end of April Indian camps all around town were hit hard. No one told them to burn the blankets of the sick or bury their dead away from their huts. In May our government ordered them to leave and by mid-June they were all gone. But I hear tell they left a trail of dead on the beaches from here to the Queen Charlotte Islands."

Katherine was appalled. "How could such a thing happen?" she blurted out. "Don't you know how to vaccinate people?"

Father glared at her. A child should not speak without being spoken to. The man looked faintly surprised but his wife smiled sadly.

"Dr. Helmcken tried his best," she said. "He managed to vaccinate at least five hundred Indians. The missionaries provided beds to die in but no vaccinations — to their everlasting shame."

"Now, Mary," said her husband, glancing apologetically at Father. "We must not speak ill of the missionaries. I'm certain they did their best."

Mary sniffed and looked away.

"You missed all the excitement in April," said the storekeeper, eager to change the subject. "Just as the *Oregon* was leaving the Esquimalt wharf, a strange woman showed up wearing a suit of gentleman's clothes. Just imagine! Trousers and all! No one could believe what they were seeing. And then, of all things, she climbed on her horse and rode *astride* it toward Victoria! It was most extraordinary, wasn't it, Mary?"

"Since you ask me, I say she shows good sense. More sense than that Laumeister fellow. Imagine bringing camels to this part of the world!"

"Camels?" asked Mrs. Harris. "Whatever for?"

"Mr. Laumeister plans to use them as pack animals to the Cariboo." Mary sniffed again. "Can you imagine, camels, in that rugged country?"

"Now, Mary," said her husband again. "I'm certain the gentleman knows what he's doing."

For the first time in weeks, Mother was smiling as they strolled back to the hotel. "It's almost civilized here," she said, "in spite of all those unruly Americans. Most people speak English and I hear they have orchestra concerts and plays and dances. And you can drink the water. I think I could be happy living here."

"Mmm," said Father, carefully avoiding her eyes.

Seeing this, Katherine's step lightened on the path and she smiled in anticipation, certain that they would not be staying long in Victoria. But then she glanced at Mother. Her smile had vanished and her mouth hardened into a bitter line as she glared at the back of her husband's head.

Two days later they were aboard the *Otter* steaming across the Strait of Georgia. They stopped at a grubby little collection of tents and wooden huts confidently named New Westminster where they boarded a small sternwheeler, the *Reliance*, for the final leg of their journey up the muddy waters of the Fraser River to Hope.

When the bow of the sternwheeler at last nudged against the shore, Katherine jumped off and scrambled up the low bank, overjoyed to be on land she would not have to leave. She looked around happily at the people who had gathered to greet the newcomers, and smiled at the prettiness of the bustling little town nestled snugly along the river bank. A jagged mountain of grey-brown rock, stark and naked against the cloudy sky, towered high above everything like the castle of a giant. As in Victoria, native people mingled with the whites and dressed in European-style clothing. She noticed, with a sense of relief, that the women were not wearing those ridiculous hoop skirts. She spotted her family gathered around an older man and ran to join them.

The man spoke with a Scottish accent. "William Charles, at your service." He tipped his hat. "I'm in charge of the Hudson's Bay fort in our wee town. Can I be of service?"

Father asked about inexpensive, temporary accommodation and Mr. Charles glanced over the five of them with a faintly baffled air. "Of course we have accommodations at the court house for single men, but for a family such as yours, let me think." He rubbed his hand over his chin.

Katherine glanced at Susan and was suddenly gripped by a cold, prickling fear. Her sister's face was white, so white it looked almost blue, and her eyes stared vacantly straight ahead. Katherine slipped an arm around her waist. Susan slumped against her until Katherine was supporting most of her weight.

"Ah, I may have just the thing," said Mr. Charles. Katherine took a half-step forward, anxious to find a place where Susan could lie down, but Mr. Charles did not move. "It's a shame," he said, "but our town is starting to die. I can see the signs already. We've been head of navigation on the Fraser since 1849, thirteen years, mind you! The Brigade Trail ends here, you realize. All the furs from New Caledonia, the Thompson, and Colville are collected here." He shook his head sadly. "Gold is the problem, bringing in all these lawless Americans. And Governor Douglas building a new road — as if he could keep them all under control!"

Katherine shifted from one foot to the other. Why did Susan just stand there, leaning on her and staring down at the road? Katherine wanted her to look up and share a joke. She wanted to ask Susan who she thought could talk longer — Mr. Charles or their father. She nudged her arm but Susan showed no interest.

At last Mr. Charles indicated that they should follow him. A row of horses loaded with furs snorted and pawed the ground outside the Hudson's Bay Company store. "Do you see?" Mr. Charles stopped beside one of the horses and ran his hand over a bundle of dark brown furs. "These are high quality furs. The best. From here they will be loaded onto a boat and shipped down to Fort Langley and Victoria."

He continued down the road, past the dirty, tired-look-ing men in their wide-brimmed hats and high boots who were unloading the furs. "Do you know the Royal Engineers have already started building the new wagon road begin-ning at Yale? Yale of all places! They plan to push the road right through the canyon to Lytton and from there to the Cariboo. Before you know it, Yale will be the head of naviga-tion on the Fraser. What will become of Hope?"

"Interesting," said Father, "but I've heard the demand for furs is dropping in Europe. Perhaps gold mining is the way of the future."

"Did you hear that?" Katherine whispered to Susan. "Yale. That's where your gold nugget comes from."

Susan made a little sound in her throat.

Mr. Charles did not answer Father, but stomped ahead until he came to a tiny, wood-frame house that looked as if it might blow down in a high wind. "Here it is," he announced. "The former occupants were store owners. They've moved on — to Yale, of course. It's nothing fancy, but the rent is cheap."

"This will do nicely," said Father. "We only expect to be here a few days, until I acquire my land."

When Mr. Charles left them, the family stepped tenta-tively into the rustic cabin. Inside, it was dark and had an unpleasant, musty smell. They clustered near the door, wait-ing for their eyes to adjust.

"How nice," said Mother sadly. She brushed a layer of dust from a wooden chair and sank onto it with a tired sigh.

"We left England for this?" George moved to the centre of the room and stood with his arms folded across his chest. The room contained one other chair, a table with a broken leg, and a stone fireplace.

Father refused to answer.

Katherine helped Susan sit down and then, hearing the musical sound of Spanish rising from the street, ran to an open rectangle in the side of the house and leaned out. She watched with interest as Mexican packers in huge hats loaded supplies onto their mules.

She smiled. She could hardly wait to get started. Doing what, she was not at all certain, but she was convinced that, whatever it might be, it would be exciting. Far better than anything stuffy old England had to offer. And in a few days she would be fourteen. Katherine brushed aside a fleeting thought — she still had found nothing she could do even half as well as her sister.

"I want you to do something for me," Susan whispered in the darkness that night. They were in the small bedroom off the kitchen, where they had to share a double bed. "Will you promise?"

"Anything," Katherine replied, glad of the opportunity. Usually it was Susan who did everything for her. "I promise."

"Good. I want you to keep this for me." She pressed something hard and cold into Katherine's hand. "I know it will bring you better luck than it will me. I just don't feel right about keeping it."

"No!" Katherine knew what it was. She tried to give it back but her sister turned away.

"You promised," Susan reminded her.

"I promised to *do* something for you, not *take* something from you."

"Keep it in a safe place," Susan pleaded, "until the day you need it. "

Katherine clutched the gold rose in her fist, wishing she had not made the promise at all. The coldness of the gold frightened her, although she did not understand why. She lay quietly, listening to her sister moan softly in her sleep, and trying to still the fear that kept her awake for most of the night.

# Chapter 3

"I simply cannot believe our luck!" Father exclaimed. He ran a few steps toward the cabin that he had brought his family to see, then stopped again to admire it. "This is exactly what we have been looking for. It is unbelievable that anyone would abandon such a perfect home after such a short stay. And just look at how much of the land is cleared of trees. We'll have crops growing in no time!"

Mother placed her hands on her thin hips and looked from the towering mountain peak to the dense evergreen forest surrounding the clearing. She studied the meadow of tall grass and the forlorn little log cabin in the centre of it. "Home, sweet home," she muttered.

Katherine glanced at her and quickly away. Her mother's eyes were filling with tears and Katherine did not want to be bothered with sadness, not today. Life here would be an endless adventure and she could hardly wait for it to begin. Not only that, but today was her birthday. One should never be unhappy on one's birthday.

Father hurried away from them, toward the door of the cabin. With a quiet sigh Susan sank down on a stump. George had already wandered off in the direction of the river. That left only Katherine to run after her father for a first look at their new home.

It was made entirely of logs cut from the property. Each log dovetailed at both ends to fit neatly at the corners. Across the front, one step up from ground level, a covered verandah ran the length of the wall. Katherine crossed it to the door and stepped inside to a large sitting room dominated by a heavy wood table and chairs cut from the stumps of trees. Two more comfortable looking chairs were set before a ceiling-high stone fireplace. She quickly explored two very small bedrooms to the right of the sitting room and, at the back, an even smaller one, no bigger than a large closet. Next to it was a crude lean-to that served as a kitchen.

In the main room Father walked to a window and tapped it with his knuckles. "Look, Kate, real glass."

"My dear, do we deserve such luxury?" The sharp voice made them both swing to face her. Small though she was, Mother loomed in the doorway, her hands still firmly attached to her hips. "Susan is feeling poorly," she said. Her voice echoed hollowly through the empty rooms. "You must help her inside, out of the hot sun."

Katherine gasped and ran outside. It could not be true. Susan had been feeling so much better in the last few days — she had almost been her old self. Mother must be saying this only to make Father feel bad.

She found Susan still sitting on the stump but slumped forward, resting her elbows on her legs. Both hands were pressed against her eyes. Katherine dropped to her knees in front of her sister. "Suz," she said, looking up, trying to see her sister's face under the brim of her large straw hat. "Tell me it isn't true. Tell me you're feeling well."

Susan dropped one hand but held the other above her eyes, shielding them, in spite of her hat. "I shall be perfectly fine," she said, squinting badly. "I'm only tired — very tired. And the sun is so awfully bright it hurts my eyes."

Katherine studied her sister and for the first time noticed the sickly, yellowish cast of her skin. Susan's eyes were black hollows sunk in a thin, emaciated face. Yes, Katherine told herself, Susan is tired. And no wonder, with her taking care of all of us for so many weeks. What she needs is a good rest and then she will be as good as new.

"Come inside," she suggested. "It's cooler in the cabin and there's a bed where you can rest." She reached for her sister's hand and was horrified at the thin, bony feel to it; the dry, papery skin felt as if it would fall apart under her fingers. She pulled Susan to her feet almost angrily. Her sister had no right to be ill.

Susan stood absolutely still. Her eyes focused on Katherine and there was a sudden look of fear in then. "I — I don't think . . ."

She swayed and Katherine reached out clumsily to catch her, but suddenly Father was there, scooping Susan up into his strong arms. "Fetch some water," he called over his shoulder, as he started toward the cabin. "Lots of it."

Katherine stood paralyzed, watching them go.

Her father, carrying Susan's limp form, had reached the verandah before Katherine finally snapped into action. Remembering a bucket she had seen in the little, lean-to kitchen, she ran into the cabin. There were two buckets, one inside the other. She grabbed them both. Shutting her ears to the hushed voices in the next room she ran outside and headed in the same direction George had gone earlier.

Katherine clambered down to the river, filled both buckets, then realized she could not make it up the bank carrying the two of them. She left one beside the river and began to pull herself up, grabbing at tree roots for handles. She stepped on the hem of her skirt and stumbled, spilling some of the water. Getting up, the toe of her boot caught in her petticoat and she crashed to her knees.

"Stupid!" she said angrily. "Why do I have to wear this stupid, long skirt? If only I were a boy I could wear trousers and do the job in half the time." She remembered the woman in Victoria who wore gentleman's clothes and wondered if she could ever be so brave.

On impulse, Katherine reached under her skirt, pulled off the ridiculous petticoat, and stuffed it under a bush. With one hand hitching her long skirt out of the way, she finally stumbled to the top, but by then the bucket was only half full. She climbed back down for the second one.

Back at the cabin she filled a cup with water and carried it to Susan where she lay on the crude pole bed. Her mother had removed Susan's dress and petticoats to make her more comfortable, but Susan's face was flushed and damp with perspiration.

Mother turned and laid her hand heavily on Katherine's shoulder to pull herself up. Their eyes met and Katherine saw the naked fear. Her stomach recoiled and she pulled away. Mother hurried from the room.

Very gently Katherine slipped her arm behind her sister's shoulders. She propped her up and lifted the cup to her lips. Susan took a tiny sip, hardly enough to wet her parched lips, and fell back exhausted. Her eyes were open but they stared blankly at the ceiling.

Mother returned with one of the buckets and two clean cloths. Dipping a cloth into the water she began to bathe Susan's burning body. Katherine wet the other one and rung it out. She placed it lightly on Susan's forehead, remembering the time on board ship when Susan had done the same for her. It had felt so good. After that Susan had helped her onto deck where a brisk, salt wind had made her feel so much better. But there was no cooling breeze here, only a blinding sun burning in a white hot sky and dry, stifling air that made breathing difficult.

Father strode into the room. "How's my girl?"

"Not at all well," Mother informed him.

"A little sunstroke, that's all it is. She'll be fine by tomorrow, wait and see."

When no one answered, Father cleared his throat. "George and I are going back into Hope for supplies."

"What?" Mother stared at him. "You would desert us in this — this wilderness?"

"We'll be back before dark. We need to pick up the rest of our belongings and sign the papers to make all of this," he swept his arm in a wide circle, "our own."

The creak of wagon wheels could be heard long after the soft plodding of the horse's hooves had faded into the distance. Katherine and her mother stayed by Susan's side, wiping her face and neck, trying to force a teaspoon of water between her cracked lips. Even that would not stay down.

The afternoon wore on but the heat did not lessen. Still the men had not returned. "Do you think you could make some tea?" Mother asked softly.

"I'll try." Katherine found some wood and got the stove going in the kitchen. She heated water in a big pot and before long she and Mother were sitting on the edge of the verandah sipping tea and eating the bread and fruit they had brought with them from Hope. The sun slid below the mountain and a faint breeze began to whisper through the trees.

"It's cooler now," said Mother. "We must bring Susan out here. Perhaps she will take some tea."

Mother went inside and Katherine, reluctant to return to the hot, stuffy cabin filled with the smell of sickness, lingered outside. She gazed up at the shadowy profile of the mountain that loomed so far above her. There would be good times, as soon as Susan got better.

Her skin froze when she heard the howl. There was no other way to describe it. A loud, animal howl filled with unbearable pain, it was coming from inside the cabin. Katherine jumped up and ran inside.

Her mother was in the tiny bedroom, sitting on the pole bed, holding Susan by the shoulders and shaking her. Susan's head flopped backward, her eyes wide and staring. Her golden hair, damp with perspiration, tumbled over her shoulders.

"Stop it, Mother, stop it!" Katherine screamed and rushed at her mother. Hardly knowing what she was doing, she gripped her mother fiercely by the shoulders and pulled her away from the bed. Mother's knees gave way. She sank to the floor, moaning pitifully and beating her fists against the rough, hard wood as though she had gone mad.

Katherine turned to her sister. She reached out to gently touch her face, still so very hot. Katherine looked into those wide blue eyes she had always envied. The eyes stared back vacantly, already glossing over. A fly landed on Susan's cheek and Katherine brushed it away angrily.

"Suz," she said, "remember how we laughed when I squashed that mosquito on your forehead?" Katherine tried to laugh now, wanting her sister to join in, wanting everything to be all right. "Remember how dirty we were? And you never complained, not once." She hugged her sister's limp body close to her chest but Susan would not move, would not respond.

"Susan!" Katherine shouted. Filled with a sudden, desperate fear she grabbed Susan by the shoulders, wanting to shake her just as their mother had done. She needed Susan to breathe, to speak, to smile again.

But suddenly she knew, she absolutely knew, that shaking her sister would do no good. A calmness came over her. Clear-headed, Katherine tried to think what Susan would have done if it were her, Katherine, who had died. As she gently laid her sister's body back on the hard bed she tried to ignore the little voice that nibbled at the edges of her mind: Susan would never have let her die.

With exquisite tenderness she closed Susan's eyes. She sat beside her beloved sister holding her hand and praying for her soul.

Katherine had no idea how long she sat there. It could have been minutes, it may well have been hours. She felt a tremendous sense of calm as she carefully placed Susan's hands, one on top of the other, across her chest. Dry-eyed, she slid onto the floor beside her mother.

Mother was moaning softly now, so filled with pain she could not hold all of it inside. Her eyes were wild and unfocused. Katherine slipped an arm around the thin shoulders. Her mother jerked away.

"Ohhh . . ." Mother moaned again, staring right through Katherine. "How could you take my Susan? My precious little Susan? My one, my perfect daughter."

Katherine pulled herself up off the floor. She walked out of the room and out of the cabin. She walked toward the river and felt, strangely, as if she were not alone. Susan walked beside her.

"She didn't mean it," Susan said. "She is too full of grief to know what she is saying. You know she loves you just as much."

"She meant it," Katherine said aloud. "If she had to choose one of us to die, she would have chosen me."

Katherine had reached the trees by then and stopped in their dark coolness. She looked down toward the river but could not see it in the gathering darkness. Her throat ached with unshed tears. "If I could have chosen, I would have chosen me too."

Then, because her knees were trembling, she sank onto the forest floor. She stretched out on her stomach and pressed her forehead against the cool earth, with her fists clenched on each side of her head. She would go to sleep and, when she awoke, this horrible dream would have ended. Susan would come looking for her, to comfort her.

# Chapter 4

"I will not stay here," Mother stated flatly. "You cannot ask that of me. It is simply too cruel."

Katherine was sitting on the edge of the verandah, curled forward, her arms wrapped around her bent knees, while her parents talked inside the cabin. The family had just returned from Susan's funeral and Katherine refused to go inside. George lurked somewhere behind her. She could hear his restless breathing but did not dare look at him.

"We have no choice," Father replied. "This is our home now, we have nowhere else to go and precious little money left. We came here to farm the land and that is exactly what we will do. We owe it to Susan . . . "

"Owe it to Susan nothing. She never wanted to come here any more than I did. If you had not forced us against our wishes to leave civilization and come to this — this colony, my precious little girl would be alive today. She would be going to balls, meeting young men, preparing for marriage as she should be. Not lying beneath the ground in this God-forsaken . . . "

"Enough! Susan wanted to come here as much as I did. She was excited by the idea of adventure. It was you, my pet, and your dear, pampered son, who wanted to remain in England."

At these words George bolted from the verandah. His

leg brushed against Katherine as he passed, and she glanced up, but he shot her such a look of disgust that she turned quickly away. It hit her then that George, like their mother, wished it had been her who died. They wished it without even knowing the real truth, that it was her fault Susan had died on Katherine's fourteenth birthday. Katherine felt sick inside. She pulled her knees closer and put her forehead down on them, wanting to make herself very small, to shrink into herself, to fold her body around the pain.

She should never have prayed to find something she could do better than Susan; and, even worse, that it happen by the day she turned fourteen. Now, too late, she realized her request was impossible to fulfill — as long as Susan were alive.

"If it weren't for Susan," Father continued, "and her tireless care, the rest of us might not have survived the voyage and you know that as well as I do. That's why I say we owe it to Susan . . . "

"I will not talk about it!"

Harsh footsteps retreated toward the back of the cabin. Katherine kept very still. Everything seemed so unreal. Her mind could not accept that she would never, for as long as she lived, see her sister's face again. The two of them would never share another secret, never laugh together, never have another argument. No, it just was not possible. Surely, if she lifted her head right now, she would see Susan walking across the clearing toward her, her long skirt swishing against the dry grasses, her blue eyes puzzled, wondering why Katherine looked so sad.

For as long as she could hold on, for as long as she did not look, Katherine could keep this dream alive. She held her head down until she convinced herself it were true, the nightmare had passed, Susan had returned. Slowly she lifted her head. Slowly, her heart pounding, she opened her eyes. The clearing was empty, shimmering in the heat of the afternoon sun. Katherine began to rock, back and forth, moaning softly.

Father stumbled onto the verandah. He stood, his face pale and haunted, staring across the land toward the jagged peak that towered above the meadow. When he spoke his voice was so low Katherine could barely hear him. "She needs us, you know. She doesn't think so right now but she does need us. You especially."

Katherine stopped rocking. She leaned forward, clutching both arms against her stomach. The words rang through her mind as clearly as if she had said them aloud. "No, Mother doesn't need me, she needs Susan. No one can replace Susan, not ever. Susan was too completely perfect." But all she said aloud was, "Yes."

Father straightened his shoulders. He spoke loudly. Too loudly. As if the sound of his own voice could chase away all unwelcome thoughts. "Katherine, do you think you could make us some tea and perhaps something to eat? Nothing much, you understand. None of us is really hungry."

"Of course." She jumped up and ran inside, glad to have a purpose.

There was little to do. The ladies of Hope had been so kind, sending out homemade pies and cold, cooked meats and freshly baked bread. Katherine made tea and laid out the food on the heavy wooden table. That done, she stepped cautiously into the back bedroom.

She expected to see her mother sprawled on the bed, beating her fists against the pain. But there she was, sitting with her back to the door, on her travel trunk, staring out the narrow window.

"Mum," Katherine said softly. "I've made tea."

Her mother made no move to answer and, thinking she had not heard, Katherine walked over and laid a hand on her shoulder. "I've made tea."

"Uhh." Mother's skin flinched at Katherine's touch, her voice was cold and hard. "How can you possibly think of food at a time like this?"

Katherine let her hand drop to her side. "I'm sorry. I just thought — I thought a cup of tea might help."

"Well it won't!" Mother snapped. "Nothing will help. Do you understand? *Nothing will help!* Not now, not ever. So go have your tea, and leave me alone."

Wringing her hands, Katherine stayed where she was. She wanted to throw her arms around her mother. She wanted to sob against her chest. She needed to be hugged; she needed to be comforted as her mother had comforted her when she was very small. More than that, she needed to confess what she had done. But her mother's back was rigid and she refused to turn her head. Katherine pressed her lips together and covered them tightly with her fingertips. It was the only way to keep from crying out. She turned and stumbled from the room.

On the verandah Father was still staring across the empty land, leaning heavily on the railing.

"The tea is ready," Katherine managed to say, "and there's food."

"Did you tell your mother?"

"Yes. She isn't hungry."

Once inside, he turned to Katherine. "Perhaps, if you take her a cup of tea, with plenty of cream and sugar, just the way she likes it . . . "

George stormed in then, in his shirt-sleeves, a foul expression on his face; he refused to look at either of them. "Has Mother eaten anything?"

"No," said Father. "Perhaps if you take her some tea . . . "

"Mm," he grunted.

After fixing Mother's tea and handing it to George, Katherine sank down at the table. Her father's fingers drummed annoyingly on the rough wood.

George returned, sat down, and helped himself to a plateful of food. "She promised to drink it, but she wants to be left alone."

Katherine picked up a slice of bread. She took one bite

and immediately felt full. So full that simply to chew and swallow without being sick took all of her concentration. She pushed her plate away. Even the smell of the food sickened her.

Slowly sipping her tea, she watched Father nibble at a piece of bread and cut a slice of meat into smaller and smaller pieces. When he had finished cutting, he stared at the meat as if trying to remember what he was expected to do with it.

George ate quickly and noisily, his gaze never rising from the table in front of his plate. When he was done he burped loudly, and wiped his mouth with his hand. He tried to push his chair back but could not because it was carved from a solid section of log. With a grunt, he stood up, dragged his long legs from under the table, and strode toward the door.

"Could you check on your mother?" Father called, but softly, as if he could make George understand without Mother overhearing in the next room. George's hesitation was so brief Katherine was not quite sure it had happened at all. Then he continued through the door and was gone.

Father turned to Katherine with hollow, empty eyes. "Kate," he whispered, "will you . . . ?"

"No!" Katherine screamed and jumped to her feet. She grabbed at the plates and cups, stacking them viciously, not caring if they broke, half wishing they would. Her whole body shook with emotion and her heart pounded heavily against her ribs. She had never defied Father before and she was afraid now to look at him. But she could not go into that room again. Not ever. How could she when her own mother could not bear the sight of her?

# Chapter 5

"What do we know about farming?" George asked. He leaned against the plough, his eyes turned toward Father yet beyond him, as if he were afraid to look directly into his face. "We've never once set foot on a farm. Although I seem to remember driving past one once in our carriage."

"Don't get smart, young man," Father snapped, "I'll have none of that. If we want to eat this winter we've got to plant now. Besides what can there be to know? You plant the seeds, you water them, the plants grow, you harvest your crop. As simple as that."

"Isn't it a little late to start planting?" asked Katherine and they both turned to stare at her. "I mean, I thought farmers planted in May."

Father's brown eyes narrowed, mocking her, reminding her she was only a child, and a girl at that. What she thought was of no importance. He sighed loudly and decided to honor her with an answer, instead of ignoring her as he usually did. Even so, Katherine knew the answer was more for George's sake than hers. "This is only the beginning of July. There is plenty of time left before the first frost. Take my word for it."

Katherine's eyes wandered over the hushed, brown field of dry grass rolling away from her. Just like the hot summer days, she thought, stretching on forever, long and dry and empty. Her father was right, there was plenty of time. Too much time. Weeks and weeks of endless days dragging toward September. The days would grow shorter and sometime, perhaps in October, there would be frost. Winter would come. But still there would be no Susan. Katherine recalled how the two of them had looked forward to escaping the rigid social rules of England: the formal dances where "well-bred" young women were put on display — like prize roses, according to Susan — so their parents could pawn them off on a suitable (the richer, the better) husband. Katherine was still too young to be involved but Susan had described to her the mindless chatter, the endless visiting, the heated discussions about who was wearing what and who was the prettiest, the most charming, debutante of the season. In England a girl was born into a certain class and remained there for life, unless she could charm or otherwise fool a man of a higher class into marrying her.

Katherine and Susan, together, had been grateful to escape that fate. They talked eagerly of the new world — the wide-open spaces, the changing seasons, the new, free life. Now Katherine would return to England in an instant, if only Susan could be restored to them. She swallowed the sob that rose in her throat and forced her mind back to the present.

Every plant needs a certain length of time to grow, even she knew that. If the time were too short, frost would destroy them before they were fit to eat. Surely, if there were certain vegetables and grains that could be planted at this time, in this part of the world, the local people would be the ones to know best. "Do you know what to plant?" she asked, her voice coming out much louder than she expected. "Did you ask anyone?"

"I've read all about it." Father did not attempt to hide his annoyance. "I know exactly what to do."

"But did you ask the local people? They're the only ones — "

"No need for that."

Katherine glanced at George, who took off his hat and wiped his forehead with the sleeve of his shirt. Gloomily he surveyed the large expanse of meadow he and Father had marked off. A few, a very few, square feet had been ploughed with the help of Duke, the horse they had purchased in Hope. Although Duke struggled valiantly, he was a riding horse, not meant to be a work horse at all.

Katherine picked up a rake. "Let's get to work."

Her father looked disapproving. "Doesn't your mother need you?"

"I scrubbed the clothes and hung them outside and washed the breakfast dishes. She's learning how to make bread. She doesn't need me for that." The truth was Mother did not want her in the cabin. Simply by being in the same room she got on her mother's nerves, Katherine knew that. No matter how hard she tried, no matter what she did, her mother would always resent her. So it was best to stay out of her way.

Anyway, there was plenty of work to do outdoors right now and Katherine preferred being outside. In the cabin Susan was always present, suffering, unable to escape her pain. Outside, Susan had all the space she needed and the freedom to move around. Susan had always loved the outdoors.

Katherine breathed the fresh, earthy scent of the soil as she bent to pick up the rocks she had raked into a pile. She tossed them into a bucket and stopped for a minute, listening to the twitterings of birds overhead, the rush of the river nearby. In the still, clear air, the craggy mountain peak loomed so close she could almost reach out and touch it.

"Suz," she whispered, "I don't understand how you did it. How did you keep George and Father from arguing all the time? How did you get Father to listen to you? We're all so miserably unhappy since you went away, we just don't know how to treat one another. I know you're watching us, I can feel you all around me. I wish you could help us. Suz? I wish we could trade places."

The hot sun beat down relentlessly as Katherine raked and picked up rocks and raked again. She paused for only a moment to remove her hat and wipe the dampness from her brow; then she stooped, lifted a full bucket of rocks in two hands, and carried it to the edge of the meadow. The rocks clattered onto the swiftly growing pile, sending up little puffs of dust. "Work hard. Don't think," every step said as she returned to the field.

By midday Katherine's petticoat had become stuck to her legs, trapping the heat, making every step a struggle between petticoat and legs. Such a ridiculous thing to wear! It was white and frilly and would take forever to wash. She watched with envy as her brother strode past in his loose-fitting trousers.

Katherine reminded herself that Susan would not have complained. Susan would have worn her petticocats even if it were only to keep Mother happy. Susan would have remained as cool and sweet-tempered as always. Why couldn't she be more like Susan?

Father and George were settled comfortably in the shade of a tree. Why were they resting at a time like this? There was so much to do. She raked a little faster, determined to finish at least this small patch before lunch. Her bucket was almost full again.

"Katherine," Father called. She looked up, tipping back the brim of her hat in order to see him. "It's lunch-time. Aren't you hungry?" He dipped a cup into the water bucket and tossed back his head to drink.

Katherine nodded. Of course she was hungry, breakfast seemed a lifetime ago. And thirsty! Her mouth was as dry as the dusty soil. She put down the rake and started eagerly toward her brother and father, pleased that they had thought to include her. She was almost there when Father lowered the cup and wiped his mouth with the back of his hand, staring at her in surprise. "Perhaps you could go and help your mother," he said. "She should have our lunch almost ready by now."

George picked up the cup, filled it, and raised it to his lips. His dark blue eyes studied her over the rim, mocking her. They seemed to be saying that she should know better than to think she could sit down with the men. She stopped and narrowed her eyes, picturing George with the water bucket turned upside down over his head. She started toward him, but stopped again. It was her job to fetch water from the river, which made water entirely too precious to waste on her brother.

Katherine turned away and trudged tiredly across the field toward the cabin. "It's not fair," she whispered to Susan, "don't they think I get tired, too? I work as hard as them, harder — they're always stopping to argue about which way the field should be ploughed, and how much they need to plough, and who is doing a better job. Why should I be the one to go and fetch the lunch?"

"Because," answered Susan, "you didn't have the good sense to be born a boy. You will pay for that mistake for the rest of your life, and there is nothing you can do about it."

The rich aroma of baking bread wafted toward her on a warm current of air. She licked her lips and walked a little faster. As she entered the cabin, a moist, suffocating heat engulfed her. In the lean-to kitchen Mother stood with her back to Katherine, looking down at the bread. There were little gobs of dough on every surface and a fine dusting of flour covered everything.

Katherine summoned up her energy. "It looks good."

Mother spun around. Her face was bright pink, damp curls clung to her forehead. "Nonsense! Have you ever seen such small loaves? It's pathetic, that's what it is. Knead the dough until it feels right, Mrs. Charles told me. Well, I kneaded it all right, I kneaded until my arms ached. How should I know when it feels right? It feels like dough to me. I never learned how to bake bread and never wanted to either."

"They may be a bit small," Katherine admitted, "but

they smell delicious. I'm sure none of us care how big the loaves are. We're too hungry to worry about that."

Katherine picked up the bread knife and started slicing a loaf. The bread was so warm and fresh it squished down until the two sides almost touched in the centre. Mother glanced at it disapprovingly before tucking it into the basket with sliced cold meat, fruit, and a large jar of tea.

"Are you coming out to have lunch with us?" Katherine asked. "It's so hot and stuffy in here, I know you would feel better outside."

Mother shook her head. She was so thin the sharp edges of her cheekbones seemed to be on the verge of breaking through the layer of skin that pulled tightly across them. Her cheeks were sunken hollows and her eyes were large, lifeless pools.

"I'm not hungry," she said tiredly. "I'm going to lie down. This afternoon I have to learn how to make butter. Can you believe that? I feel as though I'm a common dairymaid." She started out of the kitchen.

"But, Mum, you have to eat!"

Mother stopped, her back rigid. Slowly she turned and her huge eyes stared vacantly at Katherine. "I have no — " her voice broke off. Her face contorted and she turned away. "What's the use?" she muttered to herself as she ran for her bedroom.

"You see?" Katherine whispered, stepping outside, half dragging the heavy basket awkwardly with both hands. "She always does that. She turns away rather than look at me. She hates the very sight of me."

This time Susan did not answer.

They planted potatoes, carrots, onions, turnips, beets, green peas, beans, and oats. If they were lucky, the root crops would last them through the winter, stored in the root cellar the previous owners had dug deep into the earth beneath the cabin. Katherine marked each row with small sticks and every morning she ran out to examine them. She got down on her hands and knees but could see nothing. Nothing but rich, brown soil. Every day she collected water from the river and sprinkled it over the garden. In spite of Susan, and over her mother's objections, she had given up wearing petticoats in favor of a loose cotton skirt, its hem well above her ankles, so she could move about more easily.

Father and George spent days rigging up a system of ropes and pulleys on a scaffolding of logs to make it easier for her to raise buckets of water from the river. How kind of them, she thought angrily as she hauled bucket after bucket toward the garden. Now they were planning to build a well. The planning, along with the inevitable arguing, took all of their time, so the tasks of watering and weeding were left to her.

"I'm so tired," she told Susan.

"I know," her sister replied. "I would help you if I could."

One day Katherine woke up earlier than usual. Outside, the birds were singing, calling to her. She got up, dressed quickly, and ran out of the cabin while the rest of the family still slept. The early morning air was cool and clean smelling. She breathed deep, gulping breaths of it. It was soft and gentle against her cheeks. The meadow lay in the silent shadow of the mountain, which rose deep purple and craggy against the soft blue sky. Katherine made her way to the garden and dropped onto her knees. She laid her head sideways against the ground to examine the soil.

Nothing. No, wait. There was something, very tiny but definitely green. Two fine strips, thin as fir needles, no longer than her fingernail, peeked out of the ground. She worked her way along the row, her face inches from the soil. Yes, there were more of them, all along the row.

"Can you see, Susan? It's the carrots. I know you never

liked carrots very much, but this winter they may help keep us all alive."

Hearing a soft snort, Katherine raised her head. She felt eyes watching her and pulled herself up taller, still kneeling beside the garden. She scanned the meadow below. Then, in the direction of the river, she spotted him. He was sitting astride a brown horse that stood tall against the background of forest. The trees high above his head were light green now, tipped by early sunlight, but the stranger remained in shadow, quietly observing her. Katherine wondered how long he had been there.

His long hair was straight and very black. He wore no hat. His pants and shirt were soft brown and appeared to be made of animal skin. He sat easily upon his horse, watching, not moving.

Katherine hesitated, unsure whether to smile, or wave, or perhaps to look away. The young man nodded in her direction, tapped his horse with his moccasined feet, and disappeared into the woods.

# Chapter 6

Carrying a clean pail, Katherine hurried to the fenced-in area where the horse and cow were kept. She could not help but wonder if Father and George would ever get around to building the small barn they had promised. In the meantime, she tied the cow up tightly against the fence and placed the bucket beneath her udder.

Splat, splat, splat. She enjoyed the metallic sound of the first milk hitting the bucket. She loved the steady splashing sound as the bucket filled, and the warm, rich smell of milk that rose up from it.

Carrying the milk into the cabin, she placed it on the table and hurried into the kitchen to make tea. Her brother was sitting there when she returned, dipping a cup into the milk. He gulped it down noisily, then glanced at Katherine and away, as if she were not there at all. She almost laughed when she saw the line of milk on his upper lip.

"Ah, tea," he said. "And I suppose we're having porridge again?"

"Any time you want to make breakfast, you're more than welcome."

"Me?" He laughed as if she had told some enormous joke and poured himself some tea. "Bring me a bowl of that porridge before I starve to death. And I'll have some bread to go with it if you don't mind."

Katherine placed her hands on her hips and glared down at her brother. "Why don't you . . . " She wanted to tell him to quit treating her as a servant; she wanted to tell him to do something for himself for a change.

He looked up, his blue eyes half closed, arrogant. "Yes?"

She hesitated. What would Susan have done? People didn't push Susan around yet she always managed to avoid arguments. How?

"Why don't I *what*?" George asked as he stirred milk into his tea.

"Why don't you wipe that stupid milk mustache off your face?" Katherine swung around on her heel and stomped toward the kitchen.

"*If you don't mind*?" she muttered, imitating George's voice. "And what if I do mind? What then?" She grabbed a bowl from the shelf and slopped spoonfuls of hot porridge into it. She imagined the bowl smushed into George's self-important face, and saw sticky gobs of porridge dripping down his chin and onto his shirt. She pictured his half-closed, hooded eyes opened wide for once and she smiled to herself. This time she would have his full attention.

Balancing the bowl at shoulder height, Katherine half ran to the table, straight for George. He was slouched back on his seat, his fingers wrapped around the teacup. Suddenly his face went rigid, he struggled to sit up straighter, and his eyes stared helplessly as she towered over him.

"Katherine!" The voice was as clear as it was imploring. Susan's voice. "Don't do it. Please, for my sake. Can't you see he's hurting inside?"

Katherine stopped and glanced around, squinting into the dark corners of the room. Nothing. But Susan was so obviously here, so close, why couldn't she see her?

"Did you hear that?" she asked breathlessly.

George eyed the bowl of porridge hovering over his head. "What?"

"It's her, I . . . " She put the bowl down in front of George just as Father came into the room.

"Mother is feeling poorly today," he said. "She asks if you will bake the bread this morning. Perhaps you can take her a cup of tea after you get me some of that porridge."

"But . . . " Katherine tried to smile. She tried to be like Susan. Especially now, with Susan watching.

What would her sister do if they piled everything on her? How would she react if they made a servant out of her? Or — the thought suddenly struck Katherine — had they?

Father sat down and Katherine went to fill another bowl. "The carrots are coming up," she said, returning with the porridge, the last loaf of bread, and a knife. "I saw them. Perhaps you could water them today, while I make the bread?" She looked hopefully from George to Father.

"No time," said Father. "I'm heading into town right after breakfast. We need supplies."

"In that case," said George, "I'll come along with you. There's someone I need to speak with about — " He glanced up at Katherine, then over at their father. "Well, you know."

Father nodded as he sprinkled sugar over his porridge then drowned the whole mixture in fresh, warm milk.

Katherine punched down the dough with both fists. "Well, Georgie, how do you like that?" She turned the dough over, poked eyes, a nose, and a mouth in it and smashed her fist into the centre. She flattened it with the heels of her hands, folded it over, and punched it down again. "We've got to get rid of all that hot air of yours," she said. Picking up a big knife, she swung it high and sliced the dough into separate loaves. "How about that, Brother dear, does that feel good to you?"

"Katherine," said Mother, "to whom are you speaking?" She staggered, white-faced into the kitchen, clutching her empty teacup in both hands.

"No one," said Katherine. "I'm talking to myself."

"You seem to do that a lot lately."

Katherine scowled. "I suppose it's better than talking to no one."

The teacup rattled in its saucer. Mother put it down. Her lips pressed together in a crooked line as she studied Katherine. "I'm — " Her hand flew to cover her mouth and her eyes filled with tears. She looked away. "I'll finish the bread so you can get outside," she said.

Katherine walked stiffly from the room.

"Katherine?" Mother's voice was soft, an appeal.

Katherine swung around. Was it possible her mother needed her? Loved her? Her mother's face was falling apart. No. It was Susan again. Always Susan. Katherine could never compete with a perfect memory.

"Yes?" Katherine spoke more harshly than she had meant to. Her eyes narrowed, she held her head up high, knowing she looked angry but unable to stop herself.

"I — " Mother studied Katherine's face, then quickly turned her back. "I need to churn butter today. Is there enough milk?"

"Of course there is." Katherine ran outside.

The sun was beating down hard and a strong, hot wind picked up the dry soil, swirling it into the air. Little bits of grit blew into Katherine's eyes, making them hurt. The young plants would be in trouble. She had to get water right away.

She carried two buckets to the outlandish frame built by Father and George. It had two tripods made of rough logs, one set into the ground near the edge, where the bank was at its steepest. The second, smaller one, was farther back, away from the river. The tripods supported a long, slender log that reached out over the water. A rope ran the length of the log; attached by a series of loops and pulleys, it hung down from the high end and was hooked to a short post at the top of the bank.

Katherine unhooked the rope and clipped it around a bucket handle. She went to the lower end of the log, undid the other end of the rope and let it run out. The bucket lowered into the water. So far, so good. The bucket filled. She pulled in until it dangled from the high end of the log, above the river, then she secured the rope.

Now came the difficult part. Using a long pole with a hook on the end, Katherine had to grab the rope and pull in the bucket. There was nothing to keep her from falling over the bank, nothing except the single short post where the rope had been hooked. Father promised to build a railing for her one day — if she really needed it.

George had showed her how it was done. "It's simple," he'd said, in his bored but superior way. He'd reached out, from his six-foot height, and with one long arm easily snagged the bucket. He'd pulled it in, full of cool, clear water. "You see?" he'd said, looking down at her, as if daring her to object. "It's really rather simple."

"And if you were my size?"

George had looked down at her, grunted, and walked away.

Holding the pole by its very end, Katherine, at a few inches over five feet, could not reach the rope without leaning far out over the bank. She clung to the post with her left hand. With her right, she stretched out the long pole and tried to hook the rope. She could not quite reach it. She leaned out a little further. The hook slipped around the rope. Good.

"Hey!" A voice shouted behind her.

Katherine lost her footing and slipped over the edge of the steep bank. Her left shoulder wrenched painfully as it caught her weight. She swung around and grabbed the post with her right hand.

But the pole. What had happened to the pole? She heard it bounce off a rock and clatter down the bank. By the time she glanced down it was taking its final plunge into the water below. Father would be angry.

She turned back. And saw the feet.

They were clad in soft-looking, buckskin moccasins. Her

eyes travelled quickly upward. Above the moccasins were trousers, also of buckskin, which ended in a long fringe. The shirt hung loosely over the upper arms and was cut into fringes along the side seams. A graceful design painted on the front depicted a plant with long, winding stems and pointed leaves. Above that was a necklace of feathers and shells that Katherine did not recognize. Long, very black hair hung straight over broad shoulders. And then there was the face.

It was rugged with coppery-brown skin, a high forehead, prominent cheekbones, and a long, straight nose above a narrow mouth and strong chin. Clear, brown eyes looked down at Katherine: stern, unsmiling.

All this Katherine saw in a few seconds. Her heart pounded as she scrambled up the bank. Her father had told stories about the local Indian people. He said many of them were angry at the European immigrants. And why shouldn't they be? First the miners arrived and staked out claims, never once considering that the land already belonged to someone else. Then settlers came and pre-empted Crown land from the British government. The Indians, who had hunted and fished and lived on this land for thousands of years, must have been very surprised to learn that, all along, it had belonged to the Queen of England.

All these thoughts darted through Katherine's head as she drew herself to her full height and tossed her head back to look up at him. He was taller than her but not so tall as George. His arms were well muscled, not long and scrawny like her brother's. He did not speak but continued to watch her. His silence began to make her nervous.

"Look what you made me do!" she said, surprising herself. She had not meant to speak in anger. "Now how am I supposed to reach the bucket?"

He did not answer but continued to study her, as if he had never seen anything quite like her before. Nervous now, she narrowed her eyes and considered what to do. If he understood English her words would already have made him angry. If he did not, then her tone was enough to let him know she was not exactly being polite. She decided to try again.

"Listen . . . " She spoke loudly, drawing out the word, until suddenly she remembered her mother and the Spanish waiter. The problem was not his hearing, it was her language. She pointed down to the river, where the pole had fallen. She put her fingers around her throat, let her tongue loll out sideways, and bugged out her eyes. "My father," she croaked.

The young man's eyes grew wide, his black eyebrows pulled together, and he glared down at her as if she were insane. And then, suddenly, he threw back his head and laughed. With the laughter his face transformed and Katherine was startled to realize that he was probably no more than seventeen. Susan's age.

"My father also gets angry," he said, still half laughing. Then he became serious. "I have never seen a white woman so close before. You are not so ugly as the men," his mouth turned down, "all hairy and dirty. You do not smell so bad."

Katherine stared up at him and forgot all about collecting water. She was thinking instead about Susan's descriptions of the young men in England with their carefully practiced compliments. Susan told her how they vied with one another, choosing ridiculous words to tell a girl how beautiful she was. One in particular compared Susan to a delicate, golden rose, and — the thought suddenly struck Katherine — perhaps that's why Susan disliked roses so much.

"Thank you," she said, "I think," and burst out laughing.

He watched her, grinning, although not really understanding the joke. "I saw you praying to the land," he said when she stopped laughing.

"Me?" she frowned. Then she remembered how she had been on her hands and knees, how the young man on horseback had watched her from the edge of the woods. "Oh," she said, "that was you?"

He nodded.

"I wasn't praying," she explained, "I was looking for the first shoots to come up."

"Shoots?" He looked puzzled. "There is shooting from under the earth?"

"No! Oh! Not gunshots!" She suddenly realized what a confusing language English was. "I mean, new little plants. I was looking for the first, uh, the first tiny leaves to poke up out of the ground."

"And you were talking to these leaves, begging their spirits to be kind, to grow strong and healthy and feed you for the winter. This is wise."

"No. I was talking to Susan."

"Susan? This is the name of your guiding spirit?"

"No. Well, yes, in a way. Susan is my sister. She died the same day we arrived here, on the farm. But I can still feel her all around me." As she spoke, another part of Katherine stood back, amazed at herself. Amazed that she could be telling this stranger about Susan; she had not spoken of Susan to another living soul, not since the day she had died.

He looked in the direction of the cabin. "Your sister. She died here? You have not moved your home?"

It was Katherine's turn to be puzzled. "Moved?" she repeated.

"Yes, when someone dies we move away and we do not use their name for one year. This way the spirit is able to free itself from its old life. It is able to move to the spirit world where it now belongs."

"Oh," she said. "But I need my sister here."

He looked at her strangely and seemed about to speak. Then he hesitated and stared down at the river. When he spoke his voice was sad. "My sister also died. She was very young, even more young than you. White men's sickness took her and others from our village."

"I'm sorry." Katherine turned away. She did not want

to think about illness and death right now. Glancing up she saw the bucket, still swinging high over the river, and suddenly remembered the reason she was there in the first place. "The plants will die without water," she said sadly.

The young man disappeared so quickly that when Katherine peeked over the bank he was already wading into the water. He bent over and peered into the fast moving stream, motionless, watching. He moved slowly downstream. Suddenly his arm shot into the water. He stood up again with the pole in his hand. Turning, he grinned up at Katherine and waved it victoriously.

He helped her fill the second bucket and carried it toward the garden. Suddenly he stopped, staring in wonder. "Daughter of deer and pig!"

Katherine followed his gaze. "That's our cow. She gives us milk."

"How did such an animal come here?"

"From a ranch down in California. But we bought her in Hope."

He watched Katherine water the plants and seemed very curious about everything she did. She longed to ask him how he learned to speak English so well, about where he lived, and where he was going. She wanted to ask about his sister, too, but she was afraid of offending him.

"The black bear loves to dig for food," he said. "He will come in the night and eat everything. Deer will eat the leaves and flowers." He paused. "You are wise to feed the animals. Their spirits will be grateful to you."

"I'm not doing all this work to make the animals grateful," she said grumpily. "I'm doing it to keep my family alive."

"If you wish to keep all for yourself, you must build a fence."

She thought of George and Father and asked hopefully, "Have you ever built one?"

"No. I have worked for white men on pack trains. I have

learned their language but not their ways." His eyes swept across the open land. "My father does not understand fences. It hurts him to see the land cut up in this way. He believes the animals will become angry and move away."

Katherine could think of nothing to say. This land was so vast and there were so many animals it made no sense to think that a few farms scattered here and there would make any difference at all.

# Chapter 7

"You did what?" Mother's face contorted and her lower jaw trembled, but whether in fear or anger, Katherine could not be sure.

"I invited him for lunch," Katherine repeated. "He's very nice, Mother. I know you'll like him."

"A stranger? You invited a stranger into our home? I hope you at least had the good sense to tell him your father and brother are nearby."

"But they aren't. They won't be home for hours!"

Mother pressed herself up against the wall, out of sight of the open door. "Quickly, shut the door. We mustn't let him inside!"

"Oh, Mother!" Katherine picked up the bread knife. "I'll make some tea. We'll have butter and bread and some of those blueberries I picked yesterday. Do we have any left-over grouse meat? We can sit on the porch. I'm sure he'll be more comfortable outside anyway. His moccasins are wet from wading in the river to get the pole for me." Katherine gave her mother a look that clearly said, he did this for us and you begrudge him a cup of tea and something to eat?

"Hmmph!" Mother moved away from the wall, straightened her thin shoulders, and looked disapprovingly at Katherine. "It seems to me that if he had not frightened you in the first place he would not have had to climb down and fetch the pole."

Katherine sighed. Already she regretted telling her mother

what had happened. "I'm going outside and I'm taking our lunch with me." She picked up the plate of bread and butter. "I'm surprised at you, Mother. You always told me it was polite to invite people for a meal, or at least for tea."

"Oh," her mother's hands fluttered nervously, "but that was at home, in England. Not here. Not in this wilderness. Not the natives!"

"That's so stupid! What do you think he's going to do? He — " suddenly Katherine realized she did not even know the young man's name, "he's very nice." She swung around on her heel and stormed outside.

"What's your name?" she asked too loudly.

He was sitting on the step and had to twist around to see her. "White men call me William," he said.

"I am very pleased to meet you, William." She put down the plate and offered her hand. "My name is Katherine."

He reached up tentatively. The hand that shook hers was warm and very firm, quite dry to the touch. "Katherine," he repeated carefully, stretching the sound out on his tongue. She thought how pretty her name sounded the way he said it, pronouncing the 'th' halfway between the English 'th' and 'sh.' His eyes twinkled. "I am pleased to meet you, too."

Just then Mother charged through the open door, carrying a tray. On it was the teapot, cups and saucers, a sugarbowl, and a pitcher of cream. There were also three heaping bowls of blueberries. She stopped abruptly and glared down at William. Katherine, hoping her mother would at least be civil, introduced the two, formally, as she had been taught.

"I am pleased to meet you, Mrs. Harris," William said, standing up. "You are the second white woman I have met." His eyes never left her hair, which was pulled back in a bun at the nape of her neck. A few damp strands escaped and curled around her ears. He reached out tentatively to touch one.

She gasped and stepped back, clutching the tea-tray against her ribs.

William did not appear to notice. "Your hair is beautiful," he said. "It is bright gold, like the sunshine."

The hard line that was Mother's mouth softened slightly. "Why, thank you," she said and put down the tray.

Katherine smiled to herself. So, William could be clever with his compliments after all. Perhaps the young men in England could learn something from him. She chose not to dwell on his first words to her.

"Well?" she asked as William walked with long easy strides toward the woods. "Didn't I tell you that you would like him?"

Mother sniffed. "He seems nice enough, for a person of his standing."

"What do you mean, *his standing*?"

Mother's nose raised a little higher. "I simply mean that, of course, he is not English."

"No. He isn't. Neither is Governor James Douglas and you seemed to admire him well enough when he stopped by here on his way to inspect the work on the new road."

"That is an entirely different matter. Mr. Douglas is Scottish, which, everyone knows, is almost as good as English. And he's from a good class."

"Oh, Mother! Can't we leave those stupid social classes in England? They don't belong here." She paused, biting her lip. Should she say it? Yes. "By the way, isn't Mr. Douglas's wife an Indian woman?" she asked quietly.

"That is none of my affair." Mother bustled about, picking up the dishes. Katherine noted with dismay that one bowl of blueberries was still almost full. Mother barely ate a thing these days. "There are very few white women in the colony and if men are forced to look elsewhere for wives, then that's how it must be. However, when the time comes, you will have a wide choice of husbands. You must not see him again."

"Who? Governor Douglas?"

Mother pursed her lips. "Don't be impertinent, young

lady. You must not see that boy again. What would people say if they knew you were off somewhere alone in the woods with him? A young girl like you!"

"What people?" asked Katherine, squinting across the meadow, and up toward the mountainside. "There's no one here except us for miles and miles. No one to talk to. I never even get to go into Hope, like George does. William is nice and I like him. If he ever comes this way again, of course I'll talk to him. But he probably never will." Katherine stood up and ran toward the garden. It was time she did some weeding.

"I shall not tell your father about this boy," Mother called after her. "You know how he gets."

"Am I so wrong?" Katherine asked as she worked her way along the row, savagely pulling at the weeds, careful, at the same time, not to disturb a food plant. "Am I wrong to want a friend?" she asked Susan. But Susan did not answer.

Suddenly Katherine realized she had gone for several hours without once thinking of Susan. It was the first time Susan had been out of her thoughts since the dreadful day of her death. Waking and sleeping Katherine relived that day over and over, wishing she could change what happened, talking to Susan, keeping her alive in her own mind.

Nights were the worst. Trying to sleep in that same room, on that same bed. Susan was always there, silently begging for help. And Katherine lay awake for hours every night, reliving the past, wishing she could do it over — if she could do it again she would never be envious of Susan. When she finally did fall asleep, she always dreamed her sister was still with her, still alive. And that made waking up all the more painful.

What if Susan had gone now for good? What if Katherine could not bring her back? Suddenly she felt desperately alone. It was her own fault for letting her mind wander. "Mother does not like him," she went on, speaking more loudly, desperate for Susan to hear, to answer. "The way she talks, you'd think I was going to run off and marry him or something." She paused, sitting back on her heels, listening.

"Would you?" asked a quiet voice.

Katherine's heart leaped with joy. Susan had not deserted her.

"No, of course not," Katherine told her. "I only just met him. Besides, I'm only fourteen, I'm far too young to even think about marriage. You know something? I don't ever want to get married. I want always to be free."

But Susan, as usual, was the voice of reason. "You cannot live your whole life without getting married. Who would take care of you?"

"I can take care of myself. I'm pretty much taking care of this whole family right now. I do almost everything around here."

"Yes, you do. But don't forget that Father controls the money. The land belongs to him and one day George will inherit everything."

"It's not fair," said Katherine.

"No, of course not. But that's the way it is and there is nothing you can do about it."

"George is lazy and all he ever does is complain."

Susan did not answer.

"Do you like him? William, I mean. I need a friend, just one friend. Is that so wrong?"

Still Susan did not answer.


"You must teach Katherine how to shoot the rifle," Mother announced to George that evening when the family was seated at the table.

Her brother's head jerked up, his eyes darted in Father's direction.

"What?" asked Father. "Whatever for?"

"We are left here alone too often. Anyone might come by. I want Katherine to know how to shoot."

"I'll try," said George, "but she'll never be able to learn."

"Why not?" asked Katherine sharply, but George only grunted.

Reluctantly, after supper, George took down the old flint-lock rifle from above the cabin door and walked with Katherine into the meadow. He taught her how to load it through the muzzle. When she had mastered that he set up a target and showed her how to aim. She lay on her stomach and balanced the rifle with her elbows on the ground. After an hour's practice, her ears hurt from the noise, but she was shooting as well as her brother.

"Not bad," said Father, coming up behind them. "Maybe we'll have to take her hunting with us."

George grunted and walked away.

Katherine knelt by the wash bucket and scrubbed the family's clothing until her fingers were raw and bleeding. As she worked, she thought about William. Weeks had passed since the day she met him. He had entered her life and vanished as if he were no more real than a dream. She could not help wondering where he was and what he was doing. She wondered if he would ever come this way again.

As she hung the clothes in the sunshine, her eyes ran along the edge of the woods where she had first seen him. He was not there but the white shape of Duke caught her eye. He was hitched to the wagon, waiting to carry soil away, his head drooping in boredom. George and Father had finally agreed upon a location for the well and George was leaning on his shovel, watching Father dig.

Katherine's eyes swung to the garden. The feathery green carrot leaves were six inches out of the ground. Everything was growing fast in the long, hot summer days, but still there was no fence. She walked up to her mother, who was sitting on the porch, shelling peas. "Did you ever tell Father what William said about a fence?"

Mother crushed a pod between her fingers. "I did not tell Father about your Indian visitor. Can you imagine how upset he would be? But I did point out that other people have their gardens fenced."

"And?"

"You know your father. He said he would think about it when the well is finished."

"Whenever that is," Katherine mumbled, going into the cabin.

She hurried out again a few minutes later, carrying two pails. "I'm going berry picking," she announced and, without waiting for a reply, headed for the foot of the mountain.

The dry bushes rattled as she made her way up the narrow animal trail. She walked quickly. She had a long way to go. Two weeks earlier she had put the side-saddle on Duke and headed up this trail, farther than she had ever gone before, and discovered a huge crop of blackberries, almost ripe. By now they should be perfect.

They were. Bursting with juice, the fat berries filled her mouth with their warm sweetness. When Katherine had eaten her fill she set to work and in no time the first pail was almost full. She leaned forward, arms above her head, stretching to get some tempting berries that hung in the sunshine, just out of reach. Directly behind her something grunted. Her skin prickled. The vines rattled. She swallowed, turned her head slightly. Not more than twenty feet away a black bear stood on all fours, its neck outstretched. The bear's elastic lips neatly plucked a fat berry.

Slowly Katherine lowered her arms. She took one step sideways, away from the bear, then another. Her pail caught, its handle entangled in a thorny vine. When she pulled at it the bear stopped eating, sat on its haunches, and squinted toward her with its little eyes. Katherine let go of the pail which clattered to the ground and landed upright. She backed away, slowly, step by step, holding her breath. The bear watched.

She had almost reached the trail when she bumped into something. Something big, and warm, and solid. From the corner of her eye she saw that it was dark brown. Her breath caught in her throat.

It isn't a bear, she told herself. It's much too big for a bear. And it smells like — her nose twitched — horse. She turned around. The dark brown side of a horse, a leg clad in buckskin. She looked up.

Gazing down at her, his dark eyes solemn, was William. He seemed about to speak but a loud grunt from the bear caused his attention to shift. Katherine glanced back. The bear stood on its hind legs, its front paws, with their long, curving claws, waving in the empty air. Its sensitive nose twitched and it squinted toward them. The horse whinnied nervously. Its white feet danced on the trail, eager to be off.

"Give me your hand," William said calmly.

She raised her right hand, her eyes still on the bear.

"Not that one," he pushed it away impatiently. "I am told white women sit sideways on a horse. This is almost too foolish to believe. But backward?" He laughed as if he thought white people, especially white women, were ridiculous.

Katherine would not be laughed at. Her anger was quick. "Why don't you just go away and leave — " The vines rattled, too close behind her.

She threw up her left hand. William grabbed her arm and pulled her onto the horse which was already moving up the trail. Her long skirt bunched around her like a collapsed tent, the hem above the tops of her boots. She glanced over her shoulder. The bear had found the pail of berries and stuffed its nose inside.

The horse trotted up the trail, bouncing Katherine up and down while she clung tightly to William's shirt. She was already uncomfortable and had no idea where he was taking her. "You can put me down now," she said, her voice rising and falling with the movement of the horse.

William did not answer.

"I'd like to get down, please. I shall have a long enough walk home."

"What are you doing up here?" he asked.

Katherine frowned at the back of his head. "Picking berries, what do you think? I need to preserve as many as I can for winter."

"My people travel south every summer to pick berries for our winter food," William explained quietly. "We have done this for many generations. Who told you that you could gather these berries?"

"No one." Katherine was hurt by the disapproval she heard in his words, and she lashed out angrily. "How could I know the berries belong to you? Did you put up a sign?"

She needed suddenly to get away from him. "I want to go home," she said to his stiff shoulders. He gave no indication that he had heard.

The horse continued up the trail with a terrible, uneven gait that seemed to fit William perfectly. Meanwhile Katherine bounced along, going up when the horse went down and meeting it each time with a painful jolt as it came back up. As the pain grew, so did her anger.

She opened her mouth to demand that he stop right now and put her down. But just then they rounded a bend and William slowed the horse to a lovely, smooth walk. She heard voices, saw smoke rising into the still air. William took her hand to help her down and then slid off the horse himself.

In a clearing beside a trickling stream was a small collection of tents — conical shapes made from light poles bound together at the top and covered in woven mats. Masses of crushed berries dried on a large rack in the sun. On another rack, some distance away, slices of meat hung close to a fire where the smoke flowed over them. A woman knelt, placing more wood on the fire. A shower of sparks, dull in the light of day, shot upward.

The woman turned and spotted William. In one quick movement she was on her feet and hurrying toward him. She glanced briefly at Katherine and away. William greeted her warmly. He spoke quickly, nodding at Katherine as if explaining who she was. The woman studied her warily. She spoke sharply to William and William shook his head.

She was an older woman, with high cheekbones and a warm, healthy glow to her skin. She was about Katherine's height but more strongly built. Her clothing was tailored from animal skin, similar to William's except that her shirt was longer and appeared to be made from a softer material. Her shining black hair flowed straight down her back almost to her waist.

"My mother is happy to see me," William explained. "I have been away for many days working for the white men. She invites us to a meal."

"Thank you," said Katherine, smiling and nodding politely at William's mother.

They sat on the ground near one of the tents and several small children gathered about them. The children stared up at Katherine with round, curious eyes. William's mother lifted a mound of earth from the ground and a rush of steam rose out of the pit below. Out of this underground oven she lifted some meat which smelled delicious. With the meat they also ate a root vegetable soaked in oil. Katherine found it bitter and difficult to chew, but she smiled and tried to hide her dislike. There were also fresh berries and Katherine ate many of these to kill the taste of the vegetable. Her eyes flicked back and forth as William and his mother spoke. Finally he turned to Katherine.

"My mother asks where you are from."

"Tell her the farm down in the valley near the Coquihalla River."

"No," said William, frowning, "she knows this. She means before you came to this land."

"Oh. I came from England."

He waited patiently, expecting her to say more.

"England is a big island," she pointed to the east. "Over the mountains, many months travel across the land, on the other side of a great ocean. We crossed on a steamer and I was seasick the whole time."

William looked puzzled.

Katherine rocked back and forth as if she were aboard ship. She put her hands to her stomach and let her mouth fall open with her tongue hanging out.

William's mother frowned and said something to William. He answered quickly then spoke in English. "My mother worries our food has made you sick."

"Oh, no!" Katherine took her hands from her stomach. "Please tell her about England and the ship."

When he had done so his mother laughed, looking at Katherine. Katherine laughed too.

The children, having eaten, lost interest in Katherine and ran off to play. Katherine, William, and his mother continued to talk. With William interpreting she told them about her family and finally about Susan. As she spoke about her sister, her eyes filled with tears. She was surprised to see the older woman's eyes also grow moist.

When it was time to leave, William's mother presented Katherine with a beautiful, coiled basket. It was almost two feet high and just about as wide and was decorated with rows of small diamond shapes in different combinations of pale yellow, black, and red. Looking inside, she saw that it was more than half filled with berries. "Thank you," she said, smiling and bowing slightly, wishing she knew the correct words.

# Chapter 8

As soon as William's horse emerged from the end of the trail, Katherine spotted Father and George. Both were leaning on their shovels, staring at the hole that might one day be a well. Beside them, Duke appeared to be dozing.

"You can just let me off here," she said, making a move to slide off the horse's rear amid the clouds of dust that drifted up with each placing of a hoof.

But William tapped his horse lightly. "I must speak with your father."

Katherine glanced at her father and brother. They hadn't noticed her yet, there was still time. "About what?" she asked sharply.

"I need money for a new rifle." He was also looking at the men. "I can dig faster than those two."

"No!" she said too quickly, too loudly; she lowered her voice. "Please, let me off this horse before my father sees us."

The muscles of his back went rigid. He pulled on the reins. William waited as she crashed clumsily to the ground. Unsmiling, he handed down the basket. She looked up, wanting to meet his eye, to thank him. But William's mouth was set in a firm, angry line. His dark eyes avoided her.

She reached up as he handed her the pails which they had retrieved on the way home, one inside the other. "William, you don't understand . . . "

He swung the horse around, tapped it with his heels, and disappeared, leaving behind a cloud of brown dust that billowed upward in the sunlight.

Katherine stood, biting her lip, watching the dust begin to settle. He thought she was ashamed of him. Of course. She had hurt his feelings. She could not blame him for being angry. How could she explain that it was not him she was ashamed of, but her father? Father would be certain to embarrass them both, tell William that he was perfectly capable of digging his own well. But William was gone now and she would probably never see him again.

"What's going on here?"

She jumped. Slowly she turned to face him. Them.

Father was steaming toward her, his face purple, his eyes blazing. George was not far behind, his face unreadable.

"Well?" Father demanded, stopping three feet from her, with his hands jammed against his hips.

"Nothing is going on, Father. I've been berry picking. Just look at all the blackberries!" She held open the berry basket.

Her father studied the basket, ignoring the berries. "With that — that *Indian*?"

"His name is William and he is one of the Thompson people who live north of here." She hesitated and her father continued to glare. "No, I didn't go berry picking with him, I went by myself. There was a bear, and William saved my life." She decided not to mention her visit to the camp.

Father's eyes bored into the basket. George folded his arms across his chest and studied the ground near his feet.

"I see," said Father. "And he gave you a basket of berries for his trouble? He just happened to have one with him on the horse?"

"No, his mother gave me the berries as a gift." Katherine bit her lip. She had said too much already.

"Oh, well now, that explains everything. His mother was

with him on the horse? And exactly what did he do with her when you came along?"

Katherine took a deep breath. "William rescued me from the bear, but he was angry at me for picking the berries that belong to his people. After that we met his mother and she gave me some of her berries."

George shifted his weight from one foot to the other. He looked at her and shook his head, but not with his usual arrogance. It was more as if — as if he were trying to warn her of something.

Except for the visible shaking of every muscle in his body, Father did not move. He spoke calmly. "I see. So you're telling me you spent the day with this boy?"

"No, I'm — oh, Father! Aren't I allowed to have a friend?"

"A friend, yes, when you meet a nice English girl. You can't be friends with an Indian boy, it just isn't right. And, as for being alone with him, at your age — what would people think?"

Katherine was too angry to stand still. She twisted violently to the left, to the right, flinging her arms out at the empty land while words flew out of her mouth. "Do you see anyone else around here? Tell me, where am I supposed to meet a nice English girl?" She tossed her head back, glared at her father, and said in a low voice. "I like William and I would feel lucky if he'd be my friend."

George slapped his hand against his forehead.

Father narrowed his eyes. "I suppose he thinks he owns this land?"

Katherine took a slow breath to calm herself. "Owns it?" She studied him, confused. "I don't think so, not the land itself, but his village has traditional rights to the berries up there." She nodded toward the north. "I think it's the same thing with the fish in the river and the animals on the land — they have the right to harvest what they need."

Father snorted. "If I ever catch you with him again, I'll — "

He raised his hand as if to strike her.

Katherine waited, regarding him coolly through her clear, brown eyes, eyes very much like his own. Her father might storm and yell and hurl painful words at her, but he had never hit her. He had never hit any of them, not even George, whom, she thought, often deserved it.

He lowered his hand. "If he comes near you again I'll have him arrested."

Katherine gasped. Could he do that? Arrested for what? She did not know, but the thought frightened her. It was just not fair! For a moment she panicked. She had to find William, warn him to stay away. But then she remembered that William was not likely to be back, he had been so angry when he left. With a straight back and head held high she started toward the cabin.

"I will not mention this incident to your mother," he called after her. "It would upset her too much."

Katherine almost smiled. "Well, Susan," she whispered, "this has been a very interesting day."

"Now who could this be?" asked Mother a few days later.

Katherine looked up from her perch on a tree stump. She was attempting, with clumsy fingers, to darn a sock. Her mother sat on the verandah, in the shade, churning butter. A woman approached from the north, the bottom of the trail, moving gracefully in her long doeskin shirt.

Katherine recognized her at once. "She's the woman I met on the mountain, the one who gave me the berries. I guess she's come for a visit." Katherine had been unable to figure out how to tell her mother who gave her the berries without letting her know that she had seen William again. It wasn't really a lie, she reminded herself, she had simply left out a few small details.

Mother stared at Katherine in horror. "What am I supposed to do with her?"

Katherine shrugged. "I don't know. Invite her to stay for tea. What do you usually do with visitors?"

"Visitors? I barely remember the meaning of the word. Does this woman speak English?"

Katherine shook her head.

"So what are we supposed to do? Sit here and stare at each other?"

Katherine studied her mother's flushed face. Why was she so upset about such a little thing? A native woman coming to visit, for a few hours at the most. Mother seemed so lonely out here, miles from any company, you'd think she would be pleased.

"You invited her, didn't you?" her mother accused.

"No, but I . . . "

"Oh, Katherine how can you do this to me? How can you be so thoughtless? Your sister — " Mother stopped, pulled in her breath, covered her mouth with her hand.

Katherine fell apart inside but, with effort, kept her face blank. Why can't you love me? she wanted to scream. Why is everything I do wrong? How can I compete with Susan when Susan is . . . She could not add that final word, not even in her thoughts. She stood up, fixed a welcoming smile on her face, and ran to greet their visitor.

They sat on the porch, as they had done with William. Mother was gracious. She made tea and served bread with butter and blueberry jam. The other woman nodded and smiled her appreciation. She gave Mother a bundle of smoke-dried salmon.

Katherine longed to ask after William but, even if his mother could understand English, she dared not. Mother did not realize who this woman was and it was better that way.

William's mother had a message for Mother. Solemnly she held her arms in front of her and rocked them as if she were holding a baby. She raised one hand, slowly, to indicate the baby growing up. She bowed her head in deep sadness then raised up her arms to the sky. At last, clutching her hands to her chest, she pointed to Mother and back to herself. Two tears rolled down her cheeks.

Mother's lips trembled and her eyes watered. The two women had reached a common understanding. They had both lost a beloved child.

# Chapter 9

"George is never here," Mother complained one evening as Katherine and her parents sat down to supper. She stared gloomily at George's empty chair and his place, neatly set, at the table. "I don't understand that boy. Doesn't he realize we need him? How can we possibly manage without his help? And what can he be doing in town that is so important? Hope is no more than a row of crude wooden buildings on a short, dusty street."

"I expect he is making friends, meeting new people," said Father. "It's only natural. A young man needs companionship."

"Oh, and I suppose a young woman doesn't?" Katherine snapped as she spooned boiled potatoes onto the plates. Her voice echoed through the quiet room and Katherine heard the words as if they had been spoken by a stranger. Mother looked up, her lips pursed, her eyes disapproving. Father shook his head sadly.

Katherine stared at her parents. She had surprised herself as much as them. She did not understand this anger that built up so quickly inside her of late. She could not speak a kind word when she felt this way, so keyed up inside that she was about to burst. Her parents made her feel like screaming the way they were always moaning about Susan or worrying about George. It was as if she did not exist at all, not as a person, only as a servant to do the chores. If she were to disappear overnight they would first notice that their break-fast was not prepared, then they would realize their clothes were not washed, the garden not tended, the cabin floor not swept. They would reach for water and there would be none. They would scratch their heads and wonder why. Katherine sat down abruptly.

Father swallowed a mouthful of potato. "It is not the same thing."

"You are merely a child," said Mother, pushing her plate away, "not a young woman at all. When you are old enough, we will look into finding an appropriate husband for you. Until that time, we need you here."

Katherine could barely breathe. "You don't understand anything, do you? I don't want an appropriate husband one day. I want . . . I want . . . " How could she put into words what she wanted? What did she want? She barely knew. "I want a friend," she said lamely.

She looked at the boiled potatoes on her plate and her stomach revolted. She put down her fork. She stood up and walked out the door. If her parents protested, she did not hear them.

She stalked past the garden, heading toward the river. Wild and free, she thought. Wild and free. She kicked at a rock and it rolled ahead of her on the path she had worn smooth with her many trips to the river. Despite all its con-straints, she had been more free in England than she was here. At least she had had friends, games to play, and fun and laughter there. Here there was nothing but work. Work and criticism and guilt.

One day, if she were very lucky and worked very hard, she would have some appropriate man to work for, instead of her parents. She wanted to scream. She reached the end of the path and stopped suddenly, staring at, but not seeing, the far bank of the river.

"Susan," she said, "it's not what we thought it would

be. It's work and loneliness and heat and dust. You wouldn't have liked it."

Or would she? If Susan were alive, Mother would be happy. They would go into town often. They would make friends. If Susan were here, people would appear out of nowhere, as if by magic, just to be around her. Katherine was certain of that. She lowered herself to the edge of the bank, and leaned sideways against the post.

"I try to be you, Susan, but it doesn't work. I'm not good enough. I thought I could help them but I can't. They loved you too much." And me not enough, she added to herself.

"They love you too," said Susan, so quietly that Katherine barely heard. And, hearing, she did not believe.

For the first time she began to think about running away.

"But where would you go?" asked Susan.

That was the thing. Where could a young girl go? How would she survive? She could not get a job with a pack train, like William. She could not head north to search for gold. Unless — the thought grabbed at her, made her breath catch in her throat. What if she cut off her hair, dressed in George's old clothes? Would she look like a boy? Would she fool anyone? One day, perhaps, when she could not stand her life any longer, and before the appropriate man came along to seal her fate, she would do it. Meanwhile, she would keep the plan in the back of her mind. When times were tough she would bring it out, relish it, embellish it. In the meantime it would not hurt to prepare.

When at last she got to her feet, the woods were growing dark. She started toward the cabin but heard a footstep nearby, the snort of a horse. "George?" she called. There was no answer. She took a few more steps and a big, brown horse appeared suddenly in front of her.

It stopped. The rider glared down. An angry scowl made his face look mean.

"William!" she cried, pleased to see him.

William raised his head a little higher. He tapped his

horse and it began a slow walk around Katherine. The horse loomed over her. Its hot breath touched her face. She stepped in front of it. The horse stopped, so close she could see nothing but its face in the gathering darkness.

"I'm sorry," she said, "I should have introduced you to my father. It's just that I was ashamed."

There was no sound from above, only the breathing of the horse. She reached up to rub its muzzle. "You see," she continued, "he can be very embarrassing. You should have seen him in England. Whenever I had friends visiting he acted so strangely they were convinced he was insane. I wanted to die of embarrassment."

She bit her lip. She wasn't explaining very well and William was probably getting angry all over again. "The problem is," she went on recklessly, still rubbing the horse's muzzle, feeling as if she were talking to the horse, "he tries to be funny, that's the worst thing, and sometimes he tries to act as if he's my age. You can't imagine what it's like!" The horse snorted softly. "Especially," she added, "since you're only a horse and probably don't know who your father is anyway."

A loud guffaw was followed by the thud of feet hitting the ground. Then William was standing beside her, grinning.

"White men must be more strange than I thought. Why would a grown man, with the wisdom of his years, want to behave like a child? Would he not lose the respect of his people?"

"Oh, I don't think he acts that way in front of real people," she said. "Only my friends, and they were mostly girls, so they didn't really count."

William laughed.

"Where are you going?" she asked him and was suddenly afraid, remembering her father's words. She had to warn him.

"I have a job on a pack train to the Similkameen. After, I will pass through here on my return to our winter village. I must stop at the summer camp for a cache left there by my family."

"I would like to see you, " Katherine said, "when you pass through."

He nodded. "Then I will stop at your cabin."

"No!"

William eyed her strangely.

"It's my father, he doesn't want us to be friends, he said he would have you arrested if he saw you around here."

"Arrested? For what? He can do that?"

"I don't know. Maybe. He's very good at making up stories, and he has become friends with the magistrate in Hope."

"Then I will meet you here."

"How?"

"Close to the time the moon is full listen for the call of the elk." He took a hollow bone from the leather pouch which was slung over his shoulder. Bringing it to his lips he blew into it. A wild, eerie cry echoed through the woods.

The following morning George gulped down his breakfast in record time. He picked up his teacup, drained it, and replaced it heavily on the saucer. "I'm going fishing," he announced, rising abruptly.

Father glared, his eyes narrow slits. "We need to work on the well."

George looked back calmly, as if he could not see the rising anger, as if it did not exist. "Right," he said, "we'll get on that this afternoon. I'm meeting a couple of fellows at the river."

Father's face turned red. He licked his lips, his mouth opened.

"In fact," George put in quickly, "why don't you come along? I'm sure the fellows wouldn't mind. One of them is almost as old as you are."

Katherine winced. Her eyes shifted to Father. She could not believe it — he was smiling. "I don't mind if I do," he said. He took a huge gulp of his tea and pushed himself up from the table, as George had done.

They were out the door so fast neither of them heard the click of Mother's tongue against the roof of her mouth. They talked and laughed together like two little boys playing hookey. When their voices faded into the distance, Mother sighed loudly. She picked up the teapot and tipped it to pour some into her cup. The tiniest trickle dribbled out.

Katherine jumped up. "I'll make us some fresh tea," she said. Mother did not answer.

If her mother ate very little, at least she still drank tea. And with sugar and lots of cream added she was getting some small amount of nourishment. Katherine made the tea and cleared the dishes from the table, leaving the two cups and saucers, hers and Mother's. When she sat down to pour the tea she saw the lost look on her mother's face.

"She's here you know. She never really left." Katherine heard the words slip out of her mouth too late to stop them.

Mother's pale eyes regarded her blankly.

"Susan," Katherine explained. "She's still here. We talk to each other. She would talk to you, too, if you knew how to listen."

Now that she had begun, she could not stop herself. If only Mother understood about Susan, she would not be so unhappy. "Susan wants . . . " Katherine glanced at her mother and her voice fell away.

Mother's face had twisted up — like a rag when you wring the water out of it. Except for her eyes, which were large and glistening. "How could you?" her voice whispered. She pushed herself to her feet. Without another word she stumbled outside, one hand covering her mouth.

Katherine remained calmly at the table. She took a sip of her tea. "There," she said to Susan, "you see? Whenever I try to help, I end up by making things worse. I guess the only thing to do is just to keep quiet. I'll do my chores and stay out of everyone's way until the time comes."

"This may be a good thing," Susan pointed out. "You

have gotten Mother out of the cabin. Perhaps the fresh air will make her hungry."

Katherine walked to the door. She looked across the meadow and saw Mother standing beside the pile of dirt where one day a well might stand. Susan was right. Mother rarely left the cabin. It was as if she were somehow afraid that she might lose something if she went too far away, that she might not find her way back.

Katherine suddenly recognized her opportunity. Quickly she turned away from the door and hurried into the tiny cubicle at the back of the cabin where George slept. It was big enough for a narrow bed and a chest of drawers, nothing more. She pulled open the bottom drawer.

George had grown since leaving England and Mother had made new clothes for him. Mother had always been good at sewing. Although she had never made men's clothes before coming here, she had enjoyed making pretty dresses for her daughters and herself when they lived in England. She had shown both girls how to sew and Susan had learned well. Katherine was hopeless. Her stitches were big and clumsy, and the material always bunched up in an ugly way. More often than not, she had to rip out the work she had done because of some foolish mistake, such as stitching the left sleeve onto the right side of the dress. Mother and Susan set her the task of cutting the cloth but she was not even good at that. She always cut crooked and wasted so much material that Mother finally suggested she not bother trying at all.

As Katherine reached into the drawer and pulled out a pair of George's neatly folded pants, pants that were now too short for George's long legs, she wished she had shown more patience during the sewing lessons. She found two shirts that were too tight for her brother. Clutching the clothes against her chest, she ran into her room where she stuffed everything into a drawer and piled some of her own clothing on top. She would try them on tonight.

Leaving her room, she checked outside before going to rummage through Mother's sewing box. Mother was wandering down the path toward the river, staring straight ahead. Good. That would give Katherine time to find what she needed. She was on her knees looking for needles and thread when it hit her. Mother, upset and angry; leaving the cabin so quietly; walking purposefully toward the river. Mother never walked toward the river. Katherine dropped the thread and ran for the door.

Mother was no longer in sight.

"Mother!" Katherine screamed, running along the path. "Mother!" she screamed again, holding up her skirt, running as she had never run before. She reached the water rig, saw the post at the edge of the bank. No one was in sight.

Her heart pounded as she stopped at the post, touched it, looked over the bank. She closed her eyes and let out her breath, her fingers curled over the top of the post. Mother was sitting on a large rock, staring at the moving water. Katherine clambered down.

"Mother?"

Mother did not move, did not turn. Katherine wondered if she had heard. Then, "The water isn't deep enough," she said.

Deep enough for what? Katherine dared not ask. "No," she said, "the river is low. It's been a long, dry summer."

"It must be difficult for you."

Katherine hesitated. Did her mother mean collecting water or could she possibly mean life, here, in this new country? "I manage."

"Katherine, I . . . "

Katherine waited. The water tumbled over the rocks, gurgling and dimpling on its way to join the Fraser. But Mother said no more.

At last Katherine asked, "Do you think we could go into town sometime, you and I? Wouldn't you like to meet some new people?"

Mother turned then and Katherine was puzzled at the look in her eyes. Could it be fear?

"No. I'd rather not. But you must go with your father and George."

For a moment Katherine's heart lightened. Then, watching her mother turn away to gaze at the river as if mesmerized by the flowing water, Katherine felt a tingling of fear. And she knew she would never leave Mother alone on the farm.

They came home in the early afternoon, each of them holding up a string of trout, each of them smiling.

"Fish for dinner," said Father, proudly handing them to his wife.

She refused to take them. "What on earth will we do with them all?" she asked.

"We could hang them in the sun like the Indians do," said Katherine.

Three sets of eyes turned to her.

"How do you know what the Indians do?" asked Mother.

"Well, I just, I've heard. They fillet them and hang them in the sun, or in the smoke of a fire for days. Then they store them for winter."

"Let's give it a try," said George. And, to everyone's amazement he set to work, chopping kindling to begin an outdoor fire.

That evening they feasted on fish that George roasted on sticks. Katherine placed potatoes and onions near the edges of the fire and they ate these drizzled with fresh butter. Even Mother ate a little.

After dinner Katherine surprised them all with a warm blackberry pie, fresh from the oven. Later, she leaned back, watching the late shadows change the face of the rocky crag above the meadow.

"Have you forgotten me?" asked Susan, and Katherine sat up abruptly.

How dare she feel such contentment with her sister lying beneath the ground? Did Susan's life mean so little? The only way to keep her sister alive, to keep her near, was to think of her all the time. And if she were thinking of Susan, how could she possibly be so content? Katherine was alive. Susan was not. Katherine was guilty. Susan was not.

Deep shadows made every crag and ridge stand out sharply. The mountain seemed closer in this half-light, its presence somehow ominous as it loomed above them, oblivious to their presence. Lost in her own thoughts, Katherine had not been listening to the others. Gradually now, she became aware that her mother's voice had grown shrill, her father's stern, her brother's quietly pleading.

"I will not let him go! I cannot bear to lose another child!"

"You have no choice," said Father. "The decision has been made."

"You aren't losing me, Mother. I'm simply going away for a while. Just a few months, I should be back before winter is over. And we certainly need the money."

"Where are you going?" asked Katherine, but she may as well have saved her breath.

"We do," Father agreed. "I considered going myself but someone needs to be here to do the heavy work."

"Going where?" Katherine asked.

Mother snorted. "And what have you done so far? The well? The barn? A fence? George needs to be here, not traipsing off to some even more God-forsaken country than we already find ourselves in. Imagine! Going off in some vague hope of finding gold."

"Gold?" asked Katherine. "Is George going to the Cariboo?"

They all turned to her then, as if she were a stranger who had arrived in their midst unnoticed.

"Your brother is deserting us," said Mother.

"Your brother is joining a mining party, heading north to find gold."

"I'm going to a new mining town called Barkerville," George explained. "Everyone who goes there comes home rich."

"Everyone?" Katherine could scarcely believe her ears. George who loved his comforts, George who complained about the wildness of Hope, was heading off into the wilderness. "Who talked you into it?" she asked.

To her surprise, he answered her. "I'm going with friends, the fellows we went fishing with today. We have it all worked out. We've hired packers. I'm taking Duke. We'll head up the new road, stake a claim, be back in no time."

"But doesn't all that cost money?"

George avoided her eyes, glanced toward Father.

"We have a little money left," Father said, but he was looking at Mother, not Katherine. "I consider it an investment in our future."

"But," Katherine turned to George, "shouldn't you wait until spring? I mean, it's almost September. Don't most of the miners leave the north before the cold weather sets in? I thought they spent winters in Victoria."

"Next spring may be too late," said George. "We need the money to get us through this winter." He chuckled, but not in a nice way. "Do you think the little garden you spend so much time on is going to feed us?"

The anger returned, so quick and so strong she could not control it. "At least it's more than you've done! If you stayed here and caught more fish, perhaps shot a deer, or a few ducks, we could manage. Besides, we need a barn for the hay and a well in case the river freezes."

George grunted. "I'm leaving in the morning."

# Chapter 10

At first she barely noticed it, then she lay very still, listening. Yes. There it was again: a scuffling, digging sound, the "humph, humph, humph" of breath expelled. It sounded like George, grunting over some work he did not want to do. Odd, George never got up so early.

Her body jerked awake, her eyes flew open. George was gone. He'd left yesterday morning. Katherine leapt out of bed and ran outside in her night-clothes. The sun had not yet risen above the hills. Everything, from the golden-brown grass to the deep green trees, was washed with grey. The images were clear enough: the mountain starkly black against a deep blue sky, the trees by the river motionless, dark silhouettes. Katherine stopped when she saw the vegetable garden.

Standing in the middle of it, digging up huge pawfuls of carrots and munching its way through them, was a black bear. In some part of her mind Katherine knew she should run back to the cabin, wake Father, tell him to grab his gun. But all she could think of were her long hours of work and the food her family needed for winter. She yelled a loud, angry yell and ran toward the bear.

The bear looked up, chewing. It seemed vaguely surprised at this apparition charging toward it, arms flailing, white night-clothes flapping like wings. It stood up on its hind legs for a better view. Its little eyes squinted at her; its nose twitched, sniffing the air.

Consumed by anger, Katherine could not stop. If the garden failed, her summer had been wasted. She would save it or die trying. Death, if it came, would be painful perhaps but quick. No one would really care. No one except Susan. And Susan, for one, would welcome her company. And so, when the bear dropped back onto all fours, when it pawed the ground and showed its yellow teeth, Katherine was not afraid. "Get out of here, Bear!" she yelled. "Go on! Do you hear me? Get out!"

The bear's fat belly rolled from side to side as it barrelled toward her. Katherine stopped. She held her hands in front of her face, suddenly afraid. The bear leapt up, knocking her to the ground. Her breath expelled in a sudden, loud, "whomp," and the bear was on top of her.

Katherine knew then, suddenly and completely, that she did not want to die. The bear's front paws were on her shoulders, pinning her to the ground. It shook its head back and forth as if trying to decide where to bite first. The smell of its breath was almost enough to make her pass out. She had to decide: should she pretend to be dead or try to get away? But how could she possibly act dead when every muscle in her body was tense and her heart was beating like a drum against her ribs?

Just then she heard an angry bellow. The bear looked up, growled, and backed away from Katherine. It stopped and squinted up at the shovel held high above her father's head. Perhaps if he had stopped then the bear might have turned and run away, but Father was too angry.

"Stay away from my daughter!" he bellowed. The shovel came down swiftly, landing with a sickening thud on top of the bear's head. The bear staggered a little, its small eyes unfocused.

"Get into the cabin, Kate," said Father. His whole body

was shaking, with rage or fright, Katherine could not tell. Perhaps both.

"No," she scrambled to her feet, breathing heavily, "I won't leave you."

Mother came up behind her and slipped an arm around Katherine's shoulder. "We must all back away slowly," she whispered.

The bear looked at the three of them, then turned and fled. Waving the shovel in the air, Father ran after it.

"Father!" Katherine called.

"Peter!" Mother ran after her husband. "Stop! Stop this instant!"

The bear kept running and Father kept chasing. They were near the line of trees when Katherine saw something that made her heart stop. A black bear cub came wandering out of the trees, heading for its mother.

Seeing it, the bear stopped so suddenly and swung around so quickly, Father almost ran smack into her. In stopping he lowered the shovel handle until it was right in front of the bear's face. She grabbed it in her jaws.

Father, seeming at last to realize his danger, let go of the shovel and backed away. The bear tossed it on the ground and charged. Father turned and ran. The bear was upon him in no time. She knocked him to the ground and sank her teeth into the soft flesh near his shoulder.

Katherine and Mother hurried toward the horrifying scene, yelling at the bear as they ran. The cub took one look at them and retreated into the woods. There was blood everywhere. The bear still had him firmly by the shoulder and was growling, deep in her throat. Katherine picked up the shovel and slammed it down on the bear's face.

The bear let go, backed off. Mother ran to Father's side. She started to help him up but the bear, crazed by anger, charged forward and grabbed him around the leg, pulling and wrenching and shaking her head.

"Get away from him!" Katherine screamed and hit the bear on the nose. Once more the bear backed off.

Leaving her husband on the ground, Mother stood beside Katherine, shaking her fists at the bear. "Leave my family alone!" she yelled. "Haven't we been through enough?"

The bear took a few steps forward and stopped, looking up at the two of them, side by side. She shook her head dizzily, then turned and walked toward the woods where her cub had disappeared.

Mother ran to help Father to his feet. He leaned heavily on her as they started toward the cabin. Katherine walked backward behind them, holding the shovel in both hands, watching the bear waddle away, swaying from side to side. At the edge of the woods it turned and looked back, then vanished into the shadows beneath the trees.

"Katie!" her mother called and Katherine turned. Mother never called her Katie any more, not since they left England. Her mother's right arm was firmly about Father's waist, her left supported him under the elbow, but his long legs collapsed at the knees and he sank, slowly, steadily toward the ground. Katherine dropped the shovel and ran to help.

She slipped her arm around his waist, but it was no use. He collapsed, unconscious, bleeding badly from the shoulder and leg. Mother ripped strips from her petticoat and pushed them hard against the wounds. "Run and get blankets," she said to Katherine.

Even as she ran Katherine was grateful her mother had taken charge, like the mother she remembered from the old days, before they left England. She grabbed the blankets from her bed and ran back outside. By then, Father was shaking violently.

"Help me wrap a blanket around him."

They wrapped him tightly in one blanket, and, as gently as possible, rolled him onto the other one. They tried lifting him, using the blanket as a stretcher, but Mother had become so thin and frail over the last few months that she simply did not have the strength. Instead, they each took a front corner of the blanket and dragged him toward the cabin. When at last they reached the porch it was all they could do to get him up the step and inside. They laid him on the floor. Mother hurried to heat water, and Katherine ran to get pillows. Katherine dropped to her knees beside her father and gently placed a pillow under his neck and his injured shoulder, lifting it off the hard floor. She placed another under his wounded leg.

"I'm sorry, Father," she whispered and realized, with a sudden sense of shock, that her father had put his own life in jeopardy in order to save her. She stared down at him in wonder. Perhaps he did love her after all.

"What now?" she whispered. "What should I do, Susan?" After a moment she got up and ran to find her mother.

"I'm going for help," she said. "I'm going to find a doctor."

Mother wiped the perspiration from her forehead. "I need you here."

"Mother," Katherine looked from her mother's frightened eyes to her father, wrapped in blankets on the wood floor, his face as pale as death, "he needs more help than we can give him."

"But, Katherine, we don't even know if there is a doctor in Hope. And it's such a long way to walk . . . "

"It's not much more than three miles!" Katherine took a step closer to her mother. "Listen, Mother, I know you don't want to be left alone with him but I refuse to sit here and watch him die. If I can't find a doctor, I'll find someone else who can help." She started for the door.

"At least get dressed before you go," Mother called. "They'll think you've gone mad if you show up like that!"

Katherine glanced down, surprised that she was still in her night-clothes and that they were covered in blood.

She saw no one else as she ran along the final stretch of the Hudson's Bay Company Brigade Trail, holding her long skirt out of the way with one hand.

By the time she reached the quiet main street of Hope, she was staggering with fatigue. Panting heavily, she tried to focus on the small, timber-frame buildings that lined the dirt road. She grabbed a post to steady herself and catch her breath, then stepped up to the first store, intending to ask for directions to a doctor, but the door was locked. Only then did she notice the boards nailed over the windows. Many of the buildings were the same. She stopped to think. What now?

Of course. She must find Mr. Charles. She remembered where he lived from those first days they had spent in Hope. She ran toward his house and knocked on the door. "Please be home," she whispered, leaning her forehead against the cool wood.

The door was opened by Mrs. Charles. Her eyebrows pulled together as if she were puzzled. "Katherine?" she said, glancing behind her to see if anyone were with her. "Come inside."

Mrs. Charles guided her to a chair and sat her down. "What happened?"

"I'm all right," Katherine said. "It's my father, he needs a doctor."

"What happened?" Mrs. Charles repeated.

"It's my fault. A bear was digging up our garden, I tried to stop her. Father chased her and she attacked him."

As Katherine talked, Mrs. Charles hurried to a cupboard and started taking things out, placing them in a large leather bag. "I'm afraid we have no doctor," she said. "Since work on the Great North Road began everyone has been moving to Yale and the doctor is needed there because of all the accidents the men have in blasting that road through the canyon." She closed the bag. "I'll hitch up the wagon and see what I can do."

Katherine jumped to the ground before the wagon came to a complete stop and hurried into the house. Father still lay on the floor, unmoving. Mother knelt beside him, pressing a bright red cloth against his shoulder. There was a stack of blood-soaked cloths on the floor. Mother looked up, her blonde hair dishevelled, her eyes wide with fright. "There's so much blood!" she said. "It just won't stop."

"We'll soon fix that," Mrs. Charles assured her. She lifted the cloth to examine the shoulder. "Katherine," she said, "get more pillows. We've got to raise that shoulder as high as possible. And boil some water."

They propped him up until he was almost sitting. Mrs. Charles opened a packet from her bag and mixed a dried herb with the boiled water. She soaked a cloth in the mixture and pressed it against Father's shoulder. "You've got to press hard, right here, Mrs. Harris," she said, guiding Mother's hand.

Mrs. Charles moved to work on Father's leg. When the bleeding slowed she expertly wrapped a bandage tightly around it. She wrapped another around his shoulder and under his arm. The three of them together managed to lift him onto his bed and Mother covered him with clean blankets.

"You'll need to watch carefully for any sign of infection," Mrs. Charles explained. "Send for me any time if you are concerned. Change the dressings twice a day. I'll show you how, and I'll leave you enough of my ointment."

They moved to the sitting room where Katherine had placed tea and a simple meal of bread, blackberry jam, and dried salmon.

Mother ate a whole piece of bread. "I don't know how to thank you," she said to Mrs. Charles. "Where did you learn your doctoring skills?"

Mrs. Charles smiled. "It's amazing the things you learn when you have no other choice. It was an old Indian woman who showed me what to use for wounds such as your husband's, to keep the infection away. She showed me which plants to collect and how to prepare them."

"Will he be all right?" asked Katherine.

Mrs. Charles looked from Katherine to Mother. Mother nodded and Mrs. Charles spoke. "Provided he escapes infection. I suspect he will remain an invalid for a long time, perhaps most of the winter. The wounds are very deep and he has lost a lot of blood."

"Is there nothing we can do?" Mother asked.

"Simply keep the wounds clean, make certain he rests comfortably, and feed him good, meaty broth to build up his strength."

Neither Katherine nor Mother considered telling her they had no meat.

# Chapter 11

Father had not risen from his bed in four days. He was hot and feverish and Mother stayed by his side constantly, bathing him with cool cloths, dribbling fresh water between his dry lips.

Katherine sat on the verandah, mentally taking stock of their food supplies. One thing was clear: they needed more than just the few carrots the bear had not destroyed and the other vegetables still in the field. Along with their flour and oats, they had enough food to last a few months if they were careful. Without George and his enormous appetite, they had enough, perhaps, until Christmas. But, right now, they needed meat.

She pushed herself up tiredly and walked into the kitchen where a pot of thin gruel was heating on the wood stove. She picked up the wooden spoon and stirred the gruel, lifting some of it up and letting it slop back into the pot. As thin as soup, it was the only nourishment Father had taken since being injured. Yesterday she had tried adding a little warm milk, but his stomach had rejected it. Katherine put a few spoonfuls into a bowl which she carried to Father's bedside.

She hated the way he looked, so thin you could see the bones under his skin, and his face so white that his lips had a bluish tinge. He gazed up at her listlessly, his sunken eyes following her movements as she placed the bowl on the small table beside the bed. With Mother on one side and Katherine on the other, both of them careful not to touch his sore and swollen shoulder, they propped him up on pillows. Mother managed to spoon small amounts of the gruel into his mouth, waiting each time to be certain he swallowed.

Katherine studied his face, searching for some sign that he was getting better. There was none. The gruel was not enough.

His lips moved. A garbled sound came out. It sounded like, "Ahshry."

Mother glanced at Katherine across the bed, raising her eyebrows in a question. Katherine shook her head. She had no idea what he had said. He made a sound in his throat.

"What did you say?" asked Mother, leaning closer.

"I'm sorry," he whispered, groping shakily for her hand.

She gripped his hand in both of hers. "Sorry?" she asked. "For what? You saved Katherine's life. There's nothing to be sorry about."

He shook his head. His tongue showed between his teeth and his lips began moving as if he were trying to re-member how to form words. "I'm sorry I brought us here. We were happy enough in England."

Katherine's heart sank. She glared at her mother, defy-ing her to make a bitter, hurting remark. But Mother was quietly studying her hands. Katherine leaned a little closer, staring in disbelief. Could there be tears trickling down her mother's cheeks? Yes! Yet she seemed unaware of them as she held on fiercely to Father's limp hand.

"And now," he said, so softly his words were barely more than the expulsion of breath, "I may be leaving the two of you alone."

"Don't you dare!" Katherine exploded. She lowered her voice to a fierce whisper. "Don't you dare leave us alone! First Susan goes; then George wanders off. I won't let you disappear too! You can't just bring us here then drop off and forget about us. It isn't fair! Besides, you haven't finished the well yet! If you think I'm going to spend the rest of my life dragging up water with that stupid contraption you and George built — well, you'd better think again."

Mother's mouth fell open and her eyes implored Katherine to stop but Katherine was too worked up to care. She glared down at her father, his white face and pale lips as colourless as the pillow beneath his head. Could it be? No. It must have been her imagination. Father could not have smiled.

With his free hand he motioned her closer. Katherine leaned over until her ear was just above his lips. "What about the barn?" he whispered.

"That too," she said and, taking his hand, squeezed it gently. She turned and hurried out the door swallowing against the ache in her throat.

A pale, nearly full moon lingered high in the sky as Katherine stepped outside and started toward the river, clutching her father's rifle. The treetops above the river bank were dark, ragged outlines. The mountain stood black and ominous high above the meadow. Everything was quiet, peaceful, waiting for the first rays of sun to begin the day. An owl broke the silence with its haunting call as it flew home from the hunt on noiseless wings.

Early morning was the best time to find deer near the river. Katherine had seen them there often. She hoped desperately to see one today. At the same time she hoped that none would be there. She loved watching them gliding smoothly on their long legs to the river's edge, looking around with their large, gentle eyes, bending to take a drink. How could she bear to shoot one?

Yet she must. She climbed down the bank as quietly as possible, telling herself to be strong. Her father's life depended upon her. Besides, if she were willing to eat deer meat, she had to be willing to pull the trigger. It was a part of nature: one life for another.

Near the river's edge she settled quietly to wait, screened by some low bushes. "Susan," she whispered, "I know you never had to do anything like this, but please help me. If a deer comes, help me to aim well. Help me to pull the trigger."

She looked up and there it was, a healthy doe. It did not see her as it peered cautiously about. Slowly, deliberately, Katherine lifted the gun, and rested the barrel in the fork of two branches. She would not consider what was about to happen, she would simply aim and squeeze the trigger. The deer was very close. She could see its black nose, its dark eyes lined with black, the black tips to its ears, and the soft white lining inside.

"Please forgive me," Katherine said under her breath. She lined up the sights, aimed squarely at its neck, held her finger against the trigger, and took a deep breath. Then she saw the other one. It followed close behind, not quite as big as the doe. Its coat was just beginning to change from a dappled reddish-brown to the heavy, grey-brown coat of winter.

Katherine lowered the gun. She needed only one deer. And she would not shoot the mother and leave the fawn to grieve. The fawn bent to drink while the doe searched this way and that, her large eyes cautious. Suddenly her ears flicked back, her head jerked around. She made a soft, bleating sound and the two animals turned and leaped up the bank. In three long bounds they were gone.

Katherine wondered what had frightened the doe. Then she saw it. She held her breath as a magnificent buck walked toward her, along the river's edge, holding his head high. His tall, branching antlers curved forward gracefully. Katherine counted four points on each side. She watched in awe, admiring the quiet ease with which he moved through the trees that lined the river. Only when he lowered his head to drink did she remember her purpose.

She raised the gun. The buck lifted its head and looked in her direction, but did not see her through the leafy bushes. He was so close she could not miss. He was so wonderfully alive she could not shoot. But in a moment he would be gone, and she would not be given another chance. Her father would get weaker, perhaps die. The family would slowly starve. She took a deep breath, held it, aimed carefully, pulled the trigger.

The noise split through her head. The buck crumpled to the ground. "Oh," she said aloud. "I've done it, I've killed him. I'm sorry, Deer, I wish I didn't have to do it. I wish there had been another way."

Slowly she walked over and stood looking down. She crouched close to the body. Her aim had been good. The deer had died instantly. Katherine laid her hand on the warm neck. She took no pleasure in what she had done, but she was determined to make full use of the gift she had been given. Katherine ran back to the house to get a sharp knife and to tell her mother to boil water for broth. She and Mother would have roast venison and, later, venison stew. They would build a fire and dry the remainder of the meat for winter. The hide would make a warm rug for their bare floor.

"Your father looks better already," said Mother as the two of them sat down at the table after a long day's work. "His colour's better and he has fallen into a deep sleep. Do you know he has eaten two large bowls of broth since this morning? At this rate he'll be ready for soup by tomorrow. I cannot believe how much difference the deer meat has made."

Katherine said nothing. She stared down at the venison on her plate. There were also roasted potatoes, carrots, and onions. At first she thought she would not be able to eat, but then she remembered her vow not to waste any part of the deer. She sliced a piece, put it into her mouth. It was good. Delicious. She felt an immediate surge of strength, as if the deer had passed along some of its own power to her.

" . . . grateful to you," her mother was saying.

Katherine looked up. She realized then that her mother had been speaking but, lost in her own thoughts, Katherine had not heard. She wondered if she should ask Mother to repeat what she had said.

Her mother ate with relish, seeming to enjoy every mouthful. Katherine could not remember seeing her enjoy a meal as much. Mother looked up, swallowed. There was a strange look on her face, as if she wanted to say something but could not find the correct words.

"I hope you realize how much we love you," Mother said awkwardly, her eyes looking away. "I don't know what I would have done without you these past months."

Katherine stared.

"Since Susan, uh, since Susan died I've been in so much pain I didn't once think about how you were feeling." She hesitated, drew a shaky breath, and went on. "Simply to know I'll never see her again, never talk with her, never touch her face, never enjoy her lovely smile. Well, it has been torture for me." She swallowed and, with obvious effort, held her face together. "I imagine it always will be."

"Mother, you don't have to . . . "

"I just want you to know that I love you," Mother said quickly, as though the words would stick in her throat if she waited too long.

"I thought you hated me," said Katherine, not realizing at first that she had said the words out loud.

"Hated you?" Mother dropped her fork, stared at Katherine. "What? How could I? Why would you think that?"

"Because I'm not Susan. Because I lived and she died. And because I can't be your perfect daughter no matter how hard I try."

Mother's voice came out in a hollow whisper, "What do you mean, my perfect daughter?"

"That's what you said the day — the night Susan died.

Don't you remember? You pushed me away. You wanted Susan, not me." Katherine's throat ached with unshed tears, she pressed her lips together.

"If I said that, I don't remember. I was out of my mind — can you understand? Yes, Susan was my perfect daughter. I always thought of her that way. She did everything just *so*, just right. Susan was incapable of doing anything wrong. And she was so lovely, like a perfect flower, a lovely, golden rose." Tears were pouring down her mother's cheeks.

Katherine stared at her. A golden rose. "You see?" she said. Susan was perfect, I'm . . . " she bit her lip, searching for the right word. "Imperfect" didn't seem to fit. No. She needed a word that described someone who always blundered along, trying to do the right thing, trying to say the right words, but who never came even close to succeeding.

"Amazing." Mother filled the word in for her.

"Amazing?" Katherine repeated. That was definitely not the word she would have chosen.

"Yes." Mother dabbed at her eyes. "You constantly amaze me. You do things Susan would never have considered doing in a million years. You have imagination. You're not afraid to try new things, even if it does mean an occasional blunder. Do you think Susan would have gone out on her own and shot a deer? Do you think she would have chased a bear from the garden? Or brought an Indian boy home for lunch?"

Katherine grinned through her own tears.

"I love both of my daughters for themselves. Don't ever forget that, Katie. Don't ever try to be someone else, no matter how much you might admire them. I'm so sorry for what I've put you through. I have been unforgivably selfish."

Katherine could not speak. She got up from the table and went to throw her arms around her mother. This time Mother did not push her away.

The evening was cool, and darkness already setting in, as Katherine and Mother sat on the verandah looking toward the river, at the little pile of dirt that should be a well. "I may have imagination," Katherine said, "but I can't imagine how I'll finish the well and build a barn by myself."

Mother sighed. "If only George were here. We really need him now, provided we could get him to do his share of the work."

"Do you think that's possible?" asked Katherine.

"Miracles do happen. And we could always threaten not to feed him."

Katherine laughed. "That should work."

"What an odd sound," said her mother, turning her head to one side.

Katherine had not noticed it at first but it was louder now — an odd, echoing call that rang out across the meadow from the woods near the river. She realized, with a start, that it must be William. She longed to go yet she could not leave her mother right now. She could never remember them being so close before and she would not risk losing this newfound understanding. For that she was willing to risk missing William.

# Chapter 12

The moon glowed like a huge, orange fireball, rising slowly over the trees. Its light reached into Katherine's room as she folded under the hem of the long pants and stuffed them into her boots. She tucked the shirt into them, then put on the vest. Good, it came down well over her waist and cleverly disguised the fact that she was a girl quickly growing into a woman. From under her pillow, Katherine pulled the crumpled note she had written in scratchy ink: "Dear Mother and Father, Don't worry about me, there is something I have to do. I will be back in a few days. Love, Katherine."

She realized the message was brief but she could not think of anything else to say and so she spread it out on her bed, trying to smooth some of the wrinkles. Mother would be sure to see it here. Katherine did not like to sneak off like this, but her parents would never let her go if she asked their permission.

She took out the little packet of food she had hidden in a drawer. It contained bread, tea leaves, and some dried blueberries and meat. From another drawer she took a small pot, a mug, a fork, a spoon, and a sharp knife. She placed everything on a blanket, rolled it up, and tied both ends with a long piece of rope, leaving two loops long enough to slip over her shoulders.

Picking up a neatly folded handkerchief, she opened it

carefully. She placed the hard, cold lump that lay within on her palm, admiring the way it glowed in the moonlight. Then she rewrapped it and slipped it into her pocket.

She glanced around the room to see if she had forgotten anything. The hat! She had done her hair in tight braids pinned at the back of her head, but the large felt hat which she had taken from George's room came down to her eyebrows and completed her disguise. With one final glance around, she left her room, feeling very daring, dressed as she was in men's clothing.

In the silence of the night, she tiptoed through the hushed sitting room, past the ghostly shadows of the table and the stump chairs. She paused near the door and listened. Not a sound. She slipped out into the night. The door groaned softly as she closed it behind her.

She moved with long strides, for the first time in her life not encumbered by the clinging fabric of a skirt. Faster and faster she ran, not because she was afraid of being seen but because she felt so good. She turned off the path, jumped into the air, leapt over a fallen log, kicked her legs out sideways, and laughed aloud. She threw her arms in the air, simply because she could, because her hands were free, not holding a long skirt out of the way.

At the meeting place the shadows were dark under the trees. The only sound was the hollow rush of the river. William had not waited. She turned and started across the meadow at a half run. In record time she reached the bottom of the trail. "Susan," she puffed a little, starting up the slope, "I hope you aren't looking down, feeling ashamed of me. It feels really good to wear trousers. I wish you could have tried it. You might have liked it."

"Anyway," she went on after pausing to catch her breath, "I need to do this. If I meet up with any of those crazy gold miners out here, I don't want them to know I'm a girl. There's no telling what they might do. And I've got to find George,

Susan, I just have to. We need the well before winter and the barn, too, even if we do just have one cow. George needs to help for once in his life. Please, Susan, help me. Watch over me and keep me out of trouble. You've always done that for me, Susan, and I need you more than ever now, I really do."

As she continued up the trail Katherine felt very close to her sister, and she was not afraid. She walked quickly, certain that if she could only find William, he would take her with him up the Cariboo Road. He knew the way so well he could help her gain the time she needed to catch up to George. And she had Susan's gold rose nugget to pay for supplies.

Moonlight winked through the black silhouettes of overhead branches as Katherine picked her way up the dark path. She hurried past gloomy shadows lurking under silent trees. She tread softly, stopping often to listen. A rustle in the bushes ahead made her freeze. Her heart pounded, quick and loud. The darkness was too thick to see anything. The rustling stopped. She waited, all senses alert. Was it a bear? Something fat and low scuttled across the path. A raccoon. Katherine laughed and walked on.

She must have passed the blackberry patch by now, the place where William had picked her up on his horse. But she had not seen it. Bushes pulled at her arms and scratched at her face. She had to hold her hands in front of herself to push away the branches. Surely the path had not been so narrow before? Overhead the moon had vanished. The sky was deep black, sprinkled with tiny stars. Feeling her way, Katherine moved cautiously, afraid to continue, even more afraid of stopping.

"Susan," she whispered, "please don't let me be lost."

Gradually the sky became lighter. The path before her emerged from the blackness and she walked a little faster.

Soon after that she rounded a bend and stopped. The meadow stretched out toward the stream, just as before, but this time there were no tents, no smoking fires, no people. She looked around, confident he would be here. She walked toward the stream and, as she did, heard the soft whinny of a horse. She saw it then, William's horse, tied by a long rope to a small tree. William could not be far away. He must be sleeping.

Afraid that, like her brother, William would be grouchy if he woke up suddenly, Katherine did not dare go too close. She walked over to the stream and sank onto her knees beside it. There was not much water, barely more than a trickle. She cupped her hands and scooped up some of it for a drink. Then she unrolled her blanket, found the loaf of bread, and ripped off a chunk. After eating it, she drank some more water. Her eyes were heavy with the need for sleep. She splashed cold water on her face, determined to stay awake. If she fell asleep, William might wake up and leave, never seeing her.

She settled on the brown grass at the top of the bank, within sight of William's horse, waiting for William to wake up. The sky was pale blue now, the ground damp with a thin coat of dew, the world hushed, so peaceful at this hour . . .

She did not remember lying down, did not remember closing her eyes. But suddenly she opened them and knew she had fallen asleep. She sat up. William's horse was gone. She jumped to her feet and hurried to the tree. Frantic, she ran toward the trail.

"You! Stop right there!" The angry voice was behind her, near the stream. She whirled around. William, leading his horse toward her, glared at her with a scowl that made his face almost unrecognizable.

"William!" she cried. "I'm so glad you're here!"

He stopped walking and his scowl deepened. "How do you know my name, boy?"

Of course. How could she forget? He would not know her in these clothes, this hat. She whipped the hat off her head. "It's me, William. It's Katherine. I've come to find you because I need your help."

William's eyes widened as he recognized her. He looked

her up and down; his mouth opened slightly, but he did not speak.

Katherine began to feel uneasy. "What's wrong?" she blurted out. "Are you shocked because I'm dressed like a boy?"

"Yes." He rubbed a hand over his chin. "I am shocked to see you have two long legs. I am told white women sit sideways on a horse because they have little short legs." He held his hands up about two feet apart.

Her jaw dropped. She stared at his face. His lips formed a straight, firm line and yet his eyes... his eyes were all crinkled as if... she felt a grin pulling at the corners of her mouth. Seeing this, William started laughing, a laugh that began deep in his chest and was so infectious that before she knew it, Katherine was laughing with him.

When their laughter began to wear itself out, she was quick to take advantage of his good mood. "I need your help," she said again.

William's face sobered. "I have no time to dig a well."

"No. Oh! That's not why I need help. I need you to take me to George."

He shook his head. "I am not going to Fort George."

"No," she said, "not Fort George, Brother George. He's run off in search of gold."

William showed no interest in hearing about her brother. He set about lighting a small fire. "I'm hungry," he said.

They boiled water and Katherine put in some of her tea leaves. Sitting by the fire, they shared smoked salmon, dried venison, and yesterday's bread.

"Explain about Brother George," said William at last.

# Chapter 13

William sat at the top of the low bank, his knees bent, his arms resting lightly across them. His dark eyes studied the trees on the far side of the stream, then travelled downstream, away from Katherine.

Sitting beside him, her voice blending with the gurgle of the water, Katherine wondered if he were even listening as she told him about her brother. She took a deep breath. "The day after he left, a bear dug up our vegetable garden."

William's head swung round, his eyes boring into her face. "You did not build a fence. The bear must be grateful to you."

Katherine thought of the encounter with the bear. "I don't think so."

The corners of William's mouth turned down but he did not speak.

"When I saw that bear destroying all the work I had done, I was so angry I couldn't think straight. I went chasing after it."

His eyes narrowed. A crease appeared between his brows. "You chased a bear from the food he was eating?"

"She — yes. It was foolish, I know, but those vegetables were for my family, to feed us through the winter. Anyway, the bear attacked me and then, you know what? The most amazing thing happened. My father ran out to save me. He actually risked his life for me. Me!"

William observed her calmly.

"He's hurt badly, William, and it's all my fault. That's why I've got to find George. We need him now. He's going to have to do his share for once in his life. There's so much that needs to be done before winter sets in."

"You must go home," said William abruptly. "I am going north to my winter village. Travel through the canyon is dangerous. I cannot take you."

"Why not?"

"The footpaths are narrow. In some places you cannot place one foot in front of the other. The rock walls drop down to the river which roars though the gorge like wild animals who wait to chew you into pieces. Above, the walls rise straight to the sky. You would fall and be killed."

"I would not. I'm a very good climber."

"Some places you must cross on ladders made of long poles held together with vines. The poles are tied to trees and rocks at the top of the cliffs. Many people have been lost. White men don't know how to climb."

"Well," Katherine swallowed, "I'm not a white man, I'm a girl, and I could do it if I had to, but I think you're just trying to scare me. I happen to know it's not that bad any more. Governor Douglas had the path improved from Yale to Boston Bar when all those miners came rushing up from California to get rich. And last spring the Royal Engineers started work on the worst sections of the canyon. They're making it into a wagon road. So, I figure it must be really wide and not so dangerous at all."

"You have to cross narrow bridges built by my people. They swing in the wind high above the river."

"I hear there are ferries now."

William glared at her so fiercely that her first instinct was to back away. Instead, she met his stare defiantly. When he saw she was not to be intimidated, he tried another tactic. "My family expects me at our village. There is work to do. I have no time to wait for you and hold your hand when you are afraid."

**110**

"I don't need anyone to hold my hand and I won't slow you down because I won't be afraid. Besides, if you don't take me, I'll go anyway, alone. You can't stop me. I just thought I could travel more quickly with your help, that's all."

"I travel along the river your people call the Fraser as far as the Indian village of Camchin. From there I follow the river you call the Thompson. After the next river crossing I will soon arrive at my village. I go no farther."

"Fine," said Katherine, trying to sound confident. "I'm sure we will catch up with George long before that." Privately she puzzled over where Camchin could be. Her father had told her that the new road would follow the Thompson River from Lytton, cross at Cook's Ferry, and continue north.

"If we do not find him, you will be alone."

"I'm not afraid," she insisted. She babbled on, more to assure herself than to convince William. "I know we will catch up to George before then, you can't imagine how slow my brother is. I bet he stayed in Yale for days, simply lazing around, doing nothing, before he joined up with a pack train. We should overtake him before he even gets to Lytton."

"Where is this Lytton?"

"You should know that," she said. "It's the town built where the Thompson and Fraser Rivers meet."

"Camchin," William repeated.

"I can pay you," she said on impulse. "I have a gold nugget."

He looked skeptical. "Let me see."

She pulled the handkerchief from her pocket, and carefully unfolded it. The nugget shone in the first rays of sunshine as William lifted it from her palm. He rolled it between his fingers and examined it in the sunlight. "Strange," he said, "it looks like a flower." He studied Katherine's face. "I could take this gold and leave you here alone."

His face was dark against the bright sun which peeped over the treetops behind and made a golden aura around him.

She could not determine his mood. "I trust you," she replied.

"Ha!" William stuffed the nugget and handkerchief into the small leather pouch he kept slung over his shoulder, strode over to his horse, and leapt onto its back. Tapping the horse lightly with his heels, he headed downriver, away from her.

Katherine watched, her heart pounding, her breathing ragged. The hind end of the horse swayed this way and that, the black tail swished as if waving good-bye. The horse stopped under a tall pine. Reaching up, William grabbed the end of a dangling rope. Slowly he lowered something, a package. When it was at chest level, he untied the rope and secured the package on his horse. He glanced back. "You see?" he called. "Already you make me wait. And the journey has not yet begun."

Katherine picked up her blanket roll and ran to join him.

They stopped several feet from the shore of the Fraser, a great, muddy river that had recently emerged from the confines of the canyon and was now rushing headlong toward the sea.

"It's not as wide here as at Hope," observed Katherine.

"No. But it is more angry. There is not enough room for the waters to spread out so they push and shove against each other. They race to be first away from the mountains. Later, when it has more room, the river flows in peace toward the sea, like an old man who no longer feels the need to fight."

"It's too bad a young man can't be that smart," Katherine said and immediately wished she had not spoken.

"We must cross over," said William.

Katherine wasn't sure she had heard correctly. She looked across the boiling, surging water. The other side seemed very far away. "What? *Here*? Why? What's wrong with this side of the river?"

"The trail begins at Yale. It is on the other side. So we must cross."

Katherine's father had told her of people swimming

their horses across rivers, underestimating the power of the water, being swept away never to be heard from again. She wanted to ask how they would get across but was afraid William would tell her he should have left her behind, so she said nothing.

William tapped the horse and it walked to the edge of the river. Katherine's throat went dry. The horse's front feet were almost in the water when William turned him to the right and they continued upstream. Katherine watched a large log float swiftly past, rising up and disappearing in the current.

Suddenly William called out in his own language, startling her. She peeked over his shoulder. On a rock overlooking the river an old man, dressed in buckskin, was bent over a net, pulling out quivering, shining fish. At William's greeting he turned and looked down on the two of them. His long, dark hair was streaked with grey and his bright eyes studied Katherine out of a nut brown, wrinkled face.

"Get down," William said and she slid off the horse. William followed. He handed the horse's reins to Katherine.

The old man said something in quick, sharp tones.

William replied and turned to Katherine. "He asks who you are and why you are here. I said you are a young boy searching for his big brother."

The old man fired off another question.

"He asks what name you go by."

"Um, tell him, Albert." Albert, she thought, why on earth did I say that? It was the first name that came into her mind, the name of Queen Victoria's husband, the prince who had died last year. Now, she supposed, she was stuck with the name. But she didn't much feel like an Albert.

The old man eyed her strangely and Katherine pulled the hat more tightly over her forehead. She shifted uncomfortably, avoided his gaze.

William and the man talked back and forth, each gesturing with his hands. Then, seeming to have come to an agreement, William clambered down to the water's edge. He bent to examine a canoe that was pulled up against the shore.

Meanwhile the man walked straight toward Katherine. She planted her feet apart and held onto the reins as he came closer. His black eyes looked right through her. She did not move, although her instincts told her to scurry out of his way. He stepped around her and proceeded to examine the horse.

He was looking at the horse's teeth when William returned. William reached up, took his package and gun from the horse, then headed back toward the canoe, indicating Katherine should follow. With the bow pointing downstream, he slid the canoe into the river. "Get in," he said. "Pick up the paddle."

"But . . . " There was a movement behind William. The old man came up, grinning, carrying a freshly caught salmon.

"Albert," he said, and held the salmon toward her.

Katherine slipped her fingers under the gill plate. The fish was heavy but she pretended not to notice. She nodded to the man, turned, and stepped into the canoe, aware of her heart pounding furiously against her ribs. "Susan," she whispered, "it looks as though I'm about to join you. Please help me not to be afraid." She placed the salmon on the floor of the canoe, moved to the bow, and picked up the paddle from the floor. She had watched people in canoes and so knew how to hold the paddle, but nothing more.

"Good," said William. "You must paddle when I say, stop when I say, change sides when I say. I guide the canoe. Understand?"

She nodded and dipped the paddle into the water, just to get the feel of it.

"Not yet!" William yelled.

The canoe shot into the turbulent river. Katherine clenched her teeth and gripped the wooden paddle as if it could save her from drowning. The bow turned to her right. "Now," he yelled. She plunged the paddle into the waves and pulled back hard. They moved at an astonishing rate, cutting across the river on a diagonal, aiming for the opposite shore. She didn't dare look back but trusted William knew what he was doing. A huge whirlpool opened up in front of her, a deep swirling hole where anything that came too close would be sucked down. The canoe hit the edge of the whirlpool and swung abruptly to the left.

"Other side!" William yelled.

Katherine switched sides and paddled furiously, with every bit of strength she could muster. The canoe tipped sideways at a frightening angle. This is it, she thought, as the leaping water attempted to swamp the canoe. She paddled even harder, refusing to give up. Gradually the canoe righted itself, wobbled terrifyingly, and continued downstream. Katherine started breathing again, not even aware she had stopped.

Her arms ached. She looked down at the churning water, convinced that one false move on her part and both of them would be drowned. The shore looked impossibly far away. Ignoring the increasing pain in her shoulders and arms, she concentrated on paddling, first on one side, then the other, whenever William told her to switch.

A sudden wind, funnelling down the river, caught her hat and lifted it off her head. It flew up into the air like a strange bird, flapped its brim sideways, and finally landed in the water several yards downstream.

"Forget about it," William said. "Paddle."

Her hat floated swiftly away, bobbing up and down quite merrily. Minutes later the bow of the canoe grated up against the shore and Katherine scrambled forward. She jumped out and grabbed the canoe, pulling it farther on shore. "We did it!" she cried as William climbed out. She threw her arms around his neck and hugged him. "We didn't drown!" She looked up at him and stepped back, suddenly shy.

William's eyebrows raised slightly. "Of course not," he

said matter-of-factly. He pulled a long knife from the pouch at his shoulder and walked toward her, testing the blade with his thumb. "Sit down, Albert, before someone sees us. You were very foolish not to cut your hair short."

Katherine was glad of the excuse to sit because her legs seemed ready to give way underneath her. She sank to the ground and unpinned her braids. William held a braid in one hand and his knife in the other. He hacked and sawed until it came off, then he tossed the braid carelessly onto the ground. The pain brought tears to her eyes but Katherine looked away so he would not see them and think her weak.

When he was done, William stood back to admire his handiwork. Katherine reached a tentative hand up to touch her hair. It came down to her ears at the sides and partway down her neck at the back.

"Do I look like a boy now?" she asked, blinking, avoiding his eyes.

William folded his arms and studied her, shaking his head sadly. "Your skin is too pale and soft," he said with distaste.

She almost said, "I'm sorry," but changed her mind. "Can I help it if my skin is pale?" she asked him angrily. "Since when did we get to choose what we are — pale or dark, boy or girl?"

William shrugged. He picked up some damp soil near the river's edge and rubbed a little into his fingers, tossing the rest away. He smoothed his hands over her cheeks, leaving a thin sheen of brownish-grey. He stepped back and nodded in satisfaction. "Better," he said but frowned annoyingly.

"What now?"

"Your shoulders."

"What about them?"

"They slope!"

"So? What do you want them to do?"

William did not answer but strode back to the canoe.

He picked up the blanket he had used for his horse and began slashing at it with his knife. Katherine watched in alarm, wondering if this were some strange ritual of his people. He came toward her carrying two pieces of the blanket which he folded into squares about six inches long. "Put these on."

She stared at him in confusion.

"On your shoulders," he explained patiently, indicating that she should slip them inside her shirt.

Reluctantly, she placed a piece of folded horse blanket on each shoulder, feeling ridiculous, hoping they would stay in place. She wrinkled her nose. "I smell like a horse!"

William stood back to study the effect. "That is good," he said.


Carrying their provisions on their backs, they started for Yale. They had not gone far when William suddenly stopped and watched her walk away. "You gonna walk like that?" he asked.

"Like what?" She glanced over her shoulder.

"Like this," he said, walking toward her, taking tiny steps. He held his arms in close to his sides, his fingers turned out slightly. His head was bent as if he were afraid to look up.

Katherine laughed. "You look as though you're afraid of everything."

"Yes," he said. "You must not walk as if your ankles are tied together and you are afraid to look up because someone might notice you."

"Do I walk like that?" she asked in surprise.

He stepped closer to her and placed his fingers lightly under her chin. "Lift your head. Do not be afraid of the world."

She bit her lip, looking up at him. His fingers were warm and so were his eyes, looking into hers. She felt a sudden sense of joy. William dropped his hand.

"Now," he said angrily, "walk away."

Katherine glared back at him. One minute he was nice,

the next he was bossing her around. Her face burned hot with anger but before she could open her mouth, William spoke again. "The clothes are not enough. If you wish to fool people, you must also act like a boy."

So Katherine walked away, holding her head up, stretching out her legs, taking big strides, trying to imitate the way George walked.

"No!" yelled William, "You walk as if you are following the footprints of the big man of the mountains." He spoke more softly. "Make your own size steps."

Katherine practiced as they walked toward Yale and soon fell into a long, easy stride that was comfortable for her. She had to keep reminding herself not to hang her head and, on William's advice, held her arms farther from her body, pointing her elbows out instead of in. She tried to take up as much space as possible, instead of folding inward against herself, like a frightened little rabbit scurrying for its burrow.

On the outskirts of town Katherine checked the pieces of blanket on her shoulders. They felt odd but they stayed in place remarkably well.

William reached into his leather pouch. "You will need this," he said, taking the gold nugget from the handkerchief and handing it to her.

"But?"

"Take it," he said.

They walked down Yale's one street. It turned toward the river where two sternwheelers were pushed up against the shore, their bows on dry land. The town was clustered at the foot of a low hill shorn of trees. A row of wood-frame buildings, so close together they seemed to be joined, looked down the short slope to the water. Set back, to the left of the road, was a small white church and farther to the left, a smattering of wooden houses and stores, large and small, most with gabled roofs, some perched on the edge of the low river bank.

"Remember, stand up tall, hold your shoulders back, and

try to look bigger and older than you are. You've got to take charge here. Let them understand I am working for you. I know what these men are like. They will not deal fairly with an Indian and they sure as anything will not deal fairly if they know you are a girl. So, just act as if you're one of them."

"That's easy for you to say." Katherine studied a group of men standing in front of a store. Tough looking men in shirt-sleeves, their pants tucked into high boots, they looked as if they had not washed in months. Katherine was glad of the layer of dirt on her face.

# Chapter 14

As if she could avoid being seen by doing so, Katherine kept her eyes downcast, studying the dirt road in front of her feet. There was a loud cough behind her. William. She raised her eyes and focused on the entrance to the store.

"Well, what do we have here?" asked one of the men, his voice loud and taunting.

Katherine ignored him. She kept walking, head held high, shoulders back, remembering to hold her arms away from her sides, her elbows turning outward.

"Sonny," said the voice, "does your mamma know where you are?"

The others laughed. Loud, calculating laughter. Katherine trembled inside and wished William would walk beside her instead of a few steps behind where he insisted he must stay. Still, just knowing he was there was a comfort. Suddenly a huge man stepped in front of her. She stopped and looked up. He had brown, greasy hair that hung over his forehead and neck. His face needed shaving as well as a wash. His mouth opened in an evil grin that revealed an ugly row of big, yellow teeth. Katherine almost choked at the smell of him. She held her breath.

"I'm talkin' to you, boy," the man bellowed, his mean little eyes glaring down at her over a nose that was too big for his face. "Does your mamma know where you are?"

Katherine could feel all eyes on her, waiting expectantly. She took a shallow breath and looked the man directly in the eye. "My mamma would like to know where I am," she said loudly. "Unlike yours. I expect your mamma would prefer to forget she ever had you."

Loud guffaws burst out from his friends. The man's face turned red with anger. He took a step toward Katherine, and towered over her.

"Aw, leave the kid alone, Bill. He's got a sharper tongue than you'll ever have."

Reluctantly, the big man stepped aside and Katherine strode past him into the store, her heart pounding. She could feel his beady eyes boring into the centre of her back.

Inside, the floor was made of wood planks and there was a long counter, behind which the shelves were stocked with canned goods and sacks of flour, sugar, and coffee. There were jars and bottles of all sizes alongside rifles and ammunition. Stacked on lower shelves and on the counter itself were trousers, coats, and hats. The man behind the counter, leaning one elbow on it and watching her, had a large mustache and short, neatly combed hair. He wore a shirt, tie, and vest.

"Good morning, young man, and what may I do for you?"

Morning? she thought. After all that had happened was it still only morning? "I need a few supplies," she said, using the deepest voice she could muster, "for me and my guide, William, here." She nodded at William. "We'll be wanting a few days' worth of food, the two fastest horses in town, and a hat."

"Well, then, you're in luck. I just happen to have the two best horses in the entire colony right here in my yard. A couple of miners traded them for clean clothes, a few supplies, and a ticket to New Westminster. The horses were all the poor fellas had left after a season in the Cariboo."

Katherine nodded. "My guide will look at them after we get our supplies together." She set about choosing coffee, canned beans, bread, bacon, and biscuits.

"I have just the hat for you, sir," said the storekeeper. He lifted from the shelf a handsome felt hat with a wide, soft brim.

It fit perfectly.

In the fenced yard were two sleek horses, one all black except for a white stripe down its face. The other, slightly smaller, was dark brown with a black mane and tail.

"Check them over, will you, William?" she said.

Obligingly William looked at their eyes and teeth, ran his hands over their backs, and examined their legs and feet. He nodded his approval.

Katherine pulled out the gold nugget.

The storekeeper took the nugget and placed it in the palm of his hand. He rolled it around with his fingertip, frowning. "Where did you get this?" he asked suspiciously.

"From my sister Susan."

"And where did Susan get it?"

"From a couple on a steamship going to the West Indies. They said she saved their little girl's life and they wanted her to have it."

"Ah, yes — little Rose. My brother wrote me of your sister. They are most grateful to her. And your name?"

She thought of changing it then, but was afraid of getting confused, of not remembering which name to go by. "Albert," she said.

He gave her such an odd look that Katherine almost panicked. Had he guessed the truth about her? But then he smiled and held out his hand. "Pleased to meet you, Albert. Stephen Roberts here. I would very much like to meet this sister of yours one day — to thank her in person for the life of my niece."

"Susan got panama fever. She died," Katherine said abruptly. Before the man could utter a word of condolence, she went on, "Mr. Roberts, I'm trying to find my brother. Did you happen to see a tall, skinny nineteen-year-old pass through on his way to the Cariboo this past week?"

Roberts rubbed his mustache. "I see a lot of tall, thin youths pass this way. Coming home they're even thinner." He shook his head, thinking. "No, can't say as I remember any one in particular, but the only pack train that left here in the past week was three days ago. Twenty-eight loaded mules headed up the Great North Road. I told the fellows they were crazy, heading out this time of year, but you know what men are like once they get the smell of gold in their nostrils. They'll risk everything they've got, including their lives, on a chance to get rich quick."

Katherine glanced at William. "George must be with them."

"Those mules pack three hundred pounds each," said Mr. Roberts. "They can't go more than fifteen miles a day. With my horses, you'll catch up to them easily."

"Before Lytton?"

"Well, now, that depends on your luck. If all goes smoothly they should be in Lytton by — uh — tomorrow night. And I hear the road's pretty good now, almost ready for the wagons to start rolling." He closed his hand over the nugget. "Then just think of all the supplies these get-rich-quick fellows will buy from me!"

Katherine suddenly became aware of the folded blanket on her right shoulder. It was slipping and in danger of sliding down her arm. She did not look at it but lifted her shoulder high and rubbed at it, trying to work the blanket back into place.

"Sore shoulder?" asked Roberts.

"Uh — I had a bit of an accident."

"Want me to look at it? I've done a bit of doctoring in my time."

"No, it's fine, just a bit stiff, that's all." She looked at the hand holding the nugget. "Is that enough? I mean, to pay for the horses and all?"

Roberts looked again at the rose-shaped nugget. "Sure is, Albert," he told her. "Along with that fresh salmon your guide here gave me, you'll even get a little change. I'll pack it with your food in the saddle-bags that go with the horses." He started to walk away. "Sorry to hear about your sister," he said over his shoulder.

They were on the new road and had slowed their horses to pick their way up a rocky hill when William said, "You drive a hard bargain. You got two good horses, saddles, saddle-bags, and supplies. And you still got change back from that little nugget? How did you do it?"

Katherine shrugged. "I can't imagine. Maybe because of the salmon."

"Ha! What is one salmon worth? They fill the river swimming upstream."

The road, a narrow ledge blasted out of the side of a vertical rock cliff by the Royal Engineers, was strewn with rocks that had plunged straight down the cliffs. Katherine guided her horse to its edge and leaned over. Her heart stopped beating. The road seemed balanced on the very edge of existence. She looked straight down at a wild river, raging through a narrow, rocky gorge. Her horse raised its head nervously and shied away. Around the next bend Katherine had to duck under an overhanging ledge of rock. She tried to imagine what it must have been like only a year earlier, before the narrow footpath had been widened.

They stopped their horses to look down on the site of much activity. Men were working on both sides of the river. Long cables spanned the river, and there were the beginnings of wooden towers. "That must be the Alexandra Bridge," said Katherine. "My father told me about it. It should be finished by next year."

"Hm," William grunted. "My people could do it faster."

Katherine looked at him. "You mean a bridge that swings in the wind high above the river?"

He grinned. "There is great beauty in such a bridge."

"There is great terror in such a bridge," Katherine replied and they both laughed.

They found a ferry that would carry them across the river. It was little more than several logs lashed together and pulled across by cable. The horses snorted and moved their feet nervously. William and Katherine stood by their heads to hold them steady. Katherine barely dared to breathe until she stepped off the ferry again.

"Good girl, Nugget," she said, patting her horse's neck.

"*Nugget*? What kind of a name is Nugget?"

"A good name. It's either that or Rose and I don't want to call her Rose because my sister didn't like roses. What will you call yours?"

"Never thought about it."

"Well, then, how about Coal? He's so very black."

William shrugged.

In places the new wagon road narrowed until it was no more than a trail carved out of the mountainside, barely wide enough for one horse to keep its footing. Katherine let the reins hang loose, allowing Nugget to find her own way on the rough ground. The sun was low in the sky when they came to a small, grassy shelf that cut into the rock and supported a few stunted trees. A stream trickled down the mountainside behind and tumbled into the river below.

While William started a fire Katherine removed the saddle and bags from her horse. She opened a bag and took out the bread, wrapped in heavy paper. As she undid the paper, something fell onto the ground. A small cloth bag. She picked it up and opened it. Inside was Susan's rose nugget.

Katherine stared at it in disbelief. Surely this was a mistake? Yet it was wrapped so carefully and tucked securely in with the bread. Mr. Roberts must have known this would be the first parcel she would open. She wrapped her fingers around the nugget and held it against her chest. "Susan," she whispered, knowing that Mr. Roberts must have felt terrible knowing her sister had died while his niece had lived. And so he had given her this gift. A gift *for* Susan and, in a strange way, *from* her.

# Chapter 15

In a few hours they would be in Lytton. Even though they had travelled quickly, they had as yet seen no sign of George's pack train. She was beginning to worry. She had been so certain they would catch him before they reached Lytton, she had refused even to consider any other possibility. What if he had already passed through the town? What if they reached William's village and still had not found her brother?

"Please, Susan," she whispered, "I'm running out of time. Please let us catch up to George soon."

"Look at that," said William.

Katherine followed his gaze across a wide bend in the river and saw great clouds of dust billowing up from the road ahead. Men's shouts echoed down the valley.

"Thank you," she whispered, "that was quick."

"Who is this spirit you pray to?" asked William as they urged their horses to walk a little faster along the rough road.

Katherine hesitated, embarrassed that he had noticed.

"It is not your sister? That is wrong! You must let her go free."

Katherine bristled. How dare he? What right did he have to tell her how to live her life? When she spoke, her voice was as cold as ice. "At least I care about my sister."

William's face turned hard. He said something loud and quick in his own language, tapped his horse, and moved swiftly along the trail ahead of her. Katherine did not dare ask what he had said. She glared at his back, then hurried Nugget to catch up. They rode on in angry silence.

Gradually Katherine's anger began to slip away and she started to feel sorry for what she had said. She tried to think of something, some words that would make it better, but there were none. The longer the silence lasted, the more difficult it became to break, so it came as a relief when a torrent of words burst from William's lips. "You think I don't care about my little sister? When she was a baby I played with her, I picked her up when she fell — so she would not cry. She loved to run and play and she loved to laugh. She could make even our father laugh and that is not easy. She was beautiful and clever, too. She learned — " His voice broke.

Katherine glanced sideways and was astonished to see tears in William's eyes. He turned quickly away from her. "The smallpox came to our village from the people of the coast. We were lucky. Not many got sick, but my little sister was one of those who died. We moved away from the camp so her spirit would be free to travel on to the next world. It would be selfish to keep her here, where she no longer belongs."

"But how can you just let her go? How can you continue living and pretend she never existed?"

"I do not forget. Her memory travels with me. But I must not ask her to stay in this world when her spirit belongs in another."

Katherine fell silent. Is that what she was doing? Trapping Susan in a world where she did not belong? She refused to believe it. Susan wanted to be with her. Susan wanted to remain a part of the family. And look what she had just done, she had brought George's pack train in sight, just when Katherine had asked for help. It was like a miracle.

Suddenly Nugget backed toward the cliff and raised her forelegs in the air. Katherine, taken by surprise, threw her weight forward and clung tightly with her knees to keep from falling. In front of her, Coal was rearing up, too, as if both horses had suddenly gone mad. Katherine managed to turn Nugget's head, and tried to force her along the trail, but the horse, determined to turn back, headed for the edge of the cliff.

Faced with plunging headlong over the vertical cliff or retreating, Katherine stopped fighting her horse. Nugget lowered her head, put her ears back, and galloped flat out with her black mane flying as if pursued by demons. Katherine began to pull gently on the reins, afraid Nugget would break her neck if she continued at this pace. She remembered passing a widened area not far back, a flat space that filled a cleft in the steep mountainside. Exactly where it was she could not be sure, but she watched for it, hoping to turn the horse's head in time. Suddenly, sooner than she expected, it was there, coming up on her left. Using all the strength in her legs and arms she managed to turn the terrified horse off the road and into the long grass.

Nugget panted heavily, gasping for air as she raced toward the rock cliff. Katherine pulled hard on the reins and the horse reared up. When her feet hit the ground she lowered her head so abruptly Katherine was thrown forward. Her face was buried in the coarse black hair of Nugget's mane and she could feel the rapid pulse beating hotly under the skin. Slowly she eased herself backward into the saddle. She looked behind and saw William clinging to his horse as it bolted toward them, damp with sweat and frothing at the mouth. Coal reared up, whinnied, and came to a stop.

William and Katherine slid to the ground and held their horses firmly by the reins. The horses lifted their heads and sniffed the air. Their nostrils flared and they pawed the ground uneasily.

"What happened?" asked Katherine. Her breath came in quick, shallow puffs and her legs were trembling.

"I don't know," William scratched his head. "But that

pack train in front of us is not your brother's. It is headed this way and there is something very strange about it. We must hide."

They led their horses into a copse of trees at the base of the cliff and tied them securely, out of sight of the trail, then ventured back, curious to see what had frightened their horses. They crouched behind some low bushes where they could see without being seen.

Around the bend a huge animal lurched into view. It looked like an overgrown, deformed horse and its back, under an immense load, seemed to be hunched in a peculiar way, while its load swayed back and forth with every step. A man guided the beast as it moved quickly down the trail on long, crooked legs. Its huge, flat feet were bundled into ridiculous canvas shoes, but with each step it seemed to stagger slightly, as if in pain.

The animal lowered its head and squinted about viciously, sensing their presence. Its little ears stuck out sideways, its gums pulled back to reveal huge, yellow teeth. It reminded Katherine of someone. She almost laughed aloud when she remembered who — that horrid, smelly man who had confronted her at Yale.

She glanced at William, and he raised his eyebrows. "Son of horse and moose," he whispered. Then he blinked and looked back at the animal as if it were some kind of apparition that would surely vanish as quickly as it had appeared. But it was still there, larger than life, moving along at incredible speed. Worse, there were more to come. Another beast, just as ugly and even bigger, followed the first and behind it several others loped along unhappily. Their long, hairy necks nodded up and down and their dark eyes flashed this way and that as if searching for someone to bite.

A horrid stench reached Katherine's nostrils and filled her throat, making her feel sick. She covered her nose and mouth with both hands and wished she could stop breathing. William looked at her, his hands over his nose, and rolled his eyes. Just then, the horses behind them whinnied in fear. Katherine and William ran toward them.

Once the pack train had clattered into the distance and the smell had dissipated, the horses needed time to recover and to be rubbed down after their nervous flight. With gentle hands, William carefully checked their legs and feet. "They are all right," he said. "In spite of the moose-horses."

"They're camels," Katherine explained. "They come from the desert where it's hot and there is hardly any water. The land where they live is covered in sand, which is perfect for their big, flat feet because they don't sink in it."

William looked at the rugged, rocky terrain. "Even a white man should be smart enough to know this is not sand," he remarked.

"One would think so," Katherine grinned. "But some trader, I forget his name, brought them here from California where they were being tried out. He thought they would make him rich because they can carry a thousand pounds and travel twenty-five miles a day. What's more, they only need water every third day. Anyway, he figured they would be perfect. I guess he didn't know they would scare the horses."

William snorted. "Looks to me he never figured their feet were too soft for walking on rocks."

"No one said he was smart," said Katherine.

William shook his head. "Now, because of this foolish man, we must camp out one more night before Camchin."

# Chapter 16

The morning was still early when Katherine stopped her horse and looked down. Two hundred feet below, flowing from the east, the clear blue waters of the Thompson River forced their way far out into the muddy brown of the Fraser which swept down from the north. The waters pushed against each other, rose up in bubbling ridges, then finally swirled together and roared downstream to fight their way through the canyon.

William had gone to speak with his own people in Camchin. As Katherine waited for him, she watched a ragged line of dark clouds rise higher and higher in the western sky. Ahead of the clouds, thin fingers of white streaked toward the sun. She slid down from Nugget and paced back and forth. They had to catch up to George today. If they didn't, they would surely reach William's village instead. After that she would truly be on her own. She stopped pacing and looked across the river at the lonely hills. She thought of the endless miles of country where almost no one lived.

"Susan," she whispered and suddenly felt guilty, "Susan, if you don't mind, I still need you for a little while."

The bright day suddenly turned dark. Katherine glanced up. The first thin clouds passed in front of the sun and the thicker, more ominous ones that followed now covered half the sky.

William came riding up. "They were here two nights ago," he said. "They planned to be at Cook's Ferry by last night. We might catch up today, but we must hurry."

By noon thick clouds completely covered the sky and a strong wind whisked up the valley bringing cool, damp air from the coast. Katherine and William followed the Thompson on its wide swing to the north. Gradually the valley widened and the river cut less deeply into the surrounding land.

At Cook's Ferry they crossed the river. Katherine stared down at the swiftly moving water, knowing she would soon be on her own. And she surprised herself by realizing that she was not at all afraid. It was not so difficult, this travelling on horseback, and she had enough food to last for several days. Long before that she would have found her brother.

The steep mountain terrain gave way to broad, gently rolling brown hills. A few lonely yellow pines clustered here and there on the higher ridges and bunchgrass graced the lower slopes.

"This is desert land," William told her. "It is too dry here for forests to grow."

"Maybe," Katherine suggested, "those camels we saw would be happy here." As she spoke, the first drops of rain began to fall.

William looked up. "When the clouds climb over the mountains from the sea, they leave most of their burden behind. This will not last long."

The light rain soon became a deluge. "Some desert country," Katherine grumbled, peering at William through a sheet of water. Big raindrops splashed off Coal's wet rump. Rain pounded against the ground and bounced up three inches off the hard-packed soil.

"It will not rain for long," William repeated confidently.

First the distant hills then the nearby ones disappeared behind a curtain of rain. The brim of Katherine's hat caught the water and funnelled it to the back where it poured in a steady stream down her spine, but they continued on, and William kept insisting that the rain would end any minute now.

By the time William stopped his horse, the rain had slowed to a light drizzle. Katherine brought Nugget up beside him.

"We're almost there." He glanced sideways at her. The brim of her hat had collapsed over her ears and her clothes were soaked through.

She grinned. "I'm sure glad this is desert country," she said, "otherwise we might really get wet."

"You must come to my village."

Katherine shook her head, flinging water from the brim of her hat. "Thank you, but I can't. I've got to find George. I've taken too long already. My parents will be worried."

"There will be shelter, a big fire, and hot food."

Katherine hesitated. She was cold now and William's offer was tempting. But just then the sun peeped out from behind a cloud. "I'll be fine. If I stop now the rest of the day will be wasted."

William nodded. "I will show you my village. If you need help you will know how to find me."

Little puffs of vapour rose from the wet earth as they turned off the trail. At the village they both dismounted, Katherine because she felt the need to stretch her legs in their wet and clinging pants. She counted ten round dwellings built into the ground near the river's edge. From the centre of many of the rooftops a thin line of smoke threaded its way into the air. Four canoes were pulled up against the shore with a man bent over one of them. He straightened and looked toward the young people.

The man held his head high. He had a wide mouth with thin lips that turned down firmly at the corners. His long black hair was tied at the back of his head. "My father," William whispered.

Something in his voice made Katherine glance sharply at him. There was an odd expression on William's face and his eyes darted about, unable to look directly at her. He seemed suddenly shy and embarrassed and, for the first time since she had met him, unsure of himself. She thought he looked exactly the way she would look if they were at her home with her father watching.

"But," she whispered back, "he must think I'm a boy."

William shook his head. "He is not stupid. He knows who you are."

"But how?"

"Your wet clothes do not hide your secret so well."

"Oh." She had not thought of that.

On impulse, she reached into her pocket and pulled out the gold rose nugget. William stared at it, astonished. "The storekeeper back in Yale must have wanted me to have it," she explained, "because of Susan. So now I can pay you for your help."

As William did not reach for the nugget, she pressed it into his hand. "I want you to have it," she said, "for acting as my guide. Perhaps your father will be less angry when he knows you were simply doing a job."

"No. You keep your gold. It is your charm and brings you luck. You will need it. I brought you this far only to stop you from following me."

Katherine smiled. "Really? Not for the gold? Does that mean we are friends?"

"Friends?" William glanced at his father and back at her. "How can a man be friends with a girl?"

Katherine held the muscles of her face tight, refusing to let them collapse. She would not let him see how much his words hurt her. "I guess you can't," she said. "I'll be going now."

As she turned away Katherine caught a glimpse of William's father still standing beside the canoe. His arms were folded across his chest and his eyes stared away from her, across the river.

William's words rang through her head as she climbed onto Nugget and tapped her heels against the horse's wet sides: *How can a man be friends with a girl?* She pressed her lips together and narrowed her eyes as she walked her horse away from the village. Who did he think he was anyway? He was the last person on earth she'd want for a friend. In fact, she hoped she never saw him again as long as she lived.

She set off along the trail. There were several hours of daylight left and the sun felt warm on her back. She and Nugget would be dry before it was time to stop for the night. *How can a man be friends with a girl?* She urged the horse into a canter, trying to banish the words from her mind.

It was no use. She was angry and hurt and if she didn't slow down her horse was liable to twist an ankle on this rough trail. She pulled gently on the reins. About a mile further along, she could stand it no longer. Going so slowly was driving her crazy. She stopped, dismounted, and ran to the edge of the river.

"What's wrong with me, Susan? Why doesn't anyone like me?" She picked up some rocks and tossed them angrily into the water, one by one.

"You forgot this," said a voice behind her.

She swung around. William held out the gold rose nugget. "You gave me the horse. That is enough."

She stared at the nugget, not wanting it. It had brought nothing but bad luck to her.

"What I said was wrong. I am angry at my father, not at you."

She could only glare at him.

"I try to understand how it is for him," said William. "He is used to the old ways. He does not trust white people because he is afraid they will take away our land. He thinks they will destroy the fish in the rivers and the animals in the forest."

"But why would we do that? We need them as much as you do. No, it's me he doesn't like."

William shook his head. "My father did not worry when the white men came to trade for furs. He did not like the gold miners who acted as if they owned the land, but they did not stay for long. Now he sees a white girl, he sees people building fences and changing the land. He knows you are here to stay."

Katherine couldn't believe it. "But there is so much land, how could we possibly take it all? Besides, there are so few of us and we must come from so far away, we could never threaten his way of life."

"In spite of this he is afraid. He has told me I must not be friends with a white girl. He fears I will take you for my wife and turn my back on the old ways."

"Wife?" Katherine stared at his face. "Didn't you tell him we just want to be friends?"

"He does not believe this is possible." William reached for her hand, placed the nugget in it, then drew back suddenly. He climbed onto his horse. "My father is a wise man."

"But — will I ever see you again?"

"When I pass your farm I will make the elk call. Visit me if you can."

"I will." She was no longer angry as she climbed onto Nugget. "And I hope your father is wrong — about the land."

William did not answer.

They reached the trail and went their separate ways.

# Chapter 17

That night Katherine made a small fire, ate her supper, and tried not to think. Later, under the shelter of the trees and with only her horse for company, she curled up in her blanket. But her eyes refused to close. She missed William. She thought about what he had said, about them getting married. Even if they wanted to, such a thing would be next to impossible. William's father would never forgive them. And, as for her own father, that did not even bear thinking about. "Besides," she reminded herself, speaking out loud, "I never want to get married."

Even so, it was nice to know he did not hate her.

She rolled onto her back and looked up through the dark, leafy outlines of branches overhead to a dusting of stars in the ragged patch of sky. She was surprised at herself for feeling so comfortable here, as if she truly belonged in this country. A year ago she could never have imagined sleeping outside, alone, in a vast wilderness such as this. But now that she was here, it did not seem so scary at all.

The river kept up a constant beat as it tumbled past. It lulled her into a half-sleep where she dreamed she was sitting beside the Coquihalla and Susan was in the woods nearby. She tried to find her sister but she was hidden somewhere, among the trees. She called Susan's name but her voice was drowned by the noise of rushing water.

Anxious to be on her way as soon as possible, she slept very lightly and kept looking up, searching the sky, waiting impatiently for the first light of dawn. And then, finally, it arrived, turning the black sky to grey, chasing away the dark shadows. She got up, shivering in the early morning air, and started a fire to make tea and heat her last can of beans.

Several hours later, when they were back on the trail again, Nugget began to pull sideways, trying to turn herself around. With an effort, Katherine managed to force the horse forward but Nugget pranced along uneasily and laid her ears back.

"What's the matter, girl?" Katherine asked. "I hope there aren't more camels up ahead." They struggled on, horse and rider, Nugget determined to turn back, Katherine even more determined to continue forward. The sound of men's voices reached her, and soon after that the creaking of ropes and the dull plodding of footsteps. The air smelled of damp horses and men. Nugget danced sideways around the next bend, and Katherine caught her first sight of the pack train. She forced Nugget ahead until they were even with the man at the back of the line. He was small but sturdily built with a huge hat and a drooping black mustache.

"Howdy, boy," he said, raising his hand in a gesture that resembled a salute. "Where you from? You got folks around here?"

"No. I live near Hope and I've come looking for my brother, George. I think he's with this pack train. Do you know him?"

The man shrugged.

"He's nineteen, tall and skinny, and he thinks he knows everything."

The packer laughed. "We have too many of those. I never remember all the names. You're best to go look for yourself."

Katherine nodded her thanks and set out to pass the line of heavily laden mules. They seemed to stretch on forever, creeping along the narrow trail, their bulging packs weighing them down. She couldn't help but think of the camels and the loads they were able to carry. It really was unfortunate they were so cranky — and smelly.

She passed several men on horseback, but none of them even resembled George. Some of them glanced over, surprised to see a young boy passing by alone; others did not seem to notice her at all. The mules showed little interest and Nugget passed them, her head held high, ignoring the inferior beasts.

Katherine had almost reached the front of the line when she saw a tall young man ahead, sitting straight in the saddle, wearing a jacket that might be George's. She tapped Nugget's sides and moved quickly toward him. She almost called his name but decided against it. Now that she was so close, she did not want to take him by surprise. There was no telling how George might react. He might not recognize her at first, and when he did, he would probably start acting crazy because she was out here, in man's country, and dressed (how dreadfully shocking!) as a boy.

She drew even and glanced over. He was about George's age, maybe a little older, and he had dark hair and a beard. The young man glanced at her and away as if she were no more important than a piece of dust floating past.

Katherine continued on. She counted twenty-eight mules. The first three were being led by a tall, thin man riding a white horse and wearing a felt hat. A few sandy-brown curls peeked out from under the brim. Surely he was George. He had to be George. "Please, Susan, let him be George."

Katherine bit her lip. She had done it again. Without really meaning to she had spoken to Susan, pulling her back, tying her down. Well, this was not the time to deal with that. Later, when she had found George and convinced him to come home, perhaps she would find the strength to say good-bye to Susan. In the meantime she pushed the problem from her mind.

She came up beside him, looked over. "George!" she called, certain now that it was him.

The young man turned his head. Katherine's heart sank. He looked a little like her brother — he had blue eyes and a rectangular face and that same arrogant way about him — but he was definitely not George. He frowned. "Who are you?" he asked rudely.

"Albert," she told him, holding back her temper. "George Harris is my brother and I've come to find him. Do you know where he is?"

"George has a brother?" he replied stupidly.

Katherine did not answer but simply watched him. She was relieved though. At least this fellow seemed to know George.

"Funny, he never mentioned a brother. He said he had a kid sister, back in Hope. Are you sure?"

Katherine frowned. "Of what? That he's my brother? I guess I should know! It's not something you usually make a mistake about." She raised herself on the saddle to look around. "Where is he? It's important, he's needed at home because our father has been hurt — bad."

"Oh," said the young man, suddenly looking less arrogant, "sorry to hear that. George rode on ahead with a hunting party. If you hurry you should be able to catch him."

"Thank you." She tapped Nugget with her heels.

The trail was wide and smooth enough to canter. As Nugget glided along, Katherine took off her hat and let the wind blow through her short hair. The horse's power merged with her own strength and Nugget surged along, muscles stretching, legs reaching out in a long, easy stride. Katherine loved the sense of safety she experienced from riding astride the horse, instead of side-saddle as she had learned to ride in England. Reluctantly, before Nugget began to tire, she slowed the horse to a trot and put her hat back on.

Soon she would be face to face with George. Katherine

wondered if he would fix her with that superior look she knew so well, his head back, peering down his long nose at her. If he did, she would be ready for him. She would not let him make her nervous, not after coming all this way. He might not like her very much, he might wish she had died instead of Susan, but the facts could not be changed, no matter how much anyone might wish them to be different. She would talk to him, face to face (man to man, she added with a silent little laugh), and convince him to come home where he was needed instead of going off on some crazy quest to find gold. The snow would soon be falling in the north and the ground would freeze solid. How do you dig for gold in a deep freeze?

There were sounds up ahead — a rough laugh, men's voices. Katherine felt her stomach shrink. She took a deep breath and sat up straighter in the saddle. She heard the pounding of horse's hooves coming in her direction from beyond the rise of a low hill. A man's head, the head of a horse, then the entire white horse cantered into view. Duke. The rider pulled him up short.

"Who are you?" he demanded. "You aren't part of our pack train." His words were flung at her as an accusation, as if she had no right to be here.

She breathed in and out quickly and looked him in the eye. "Hello, George," she said, "I'm Albert, your brother."

George's mouth dropped open. He stared at her, lowering his head and turning it sideways to see her face better, below the brim of her hat. "Katherine? Good God!" He glanced over his shoulder. "What if . . . it's a good thing I'm heading back alone for ammunition. What on earth are you doing here? This is no place for a girl!"

"So I've heard," she said. "It seems not many places are. Which is why I have decided to become a boy."

"Do you think you'll fool anyone with that ridiculous disguise? What's the matter with you anyway? Why aren't you at home where you belong?"

"All right," she kept her voice calm, "you've asked me three questions. I hope you will be quiet long enough for me to answer them. First: yes, I think I'll fool people who don't know me. I already have. How do you think I got this far? Second: nothing's the matter with me except that I don't think I can build a barn and dig a well by myself before winter. Which brings us to your third question. I'm here because Mother and Father need you at home. Father had an accident — he's all right — but he'll be an invalid for a long time. So, I came to get you. Besides," she added as an afterthought, "I know they miss you. Mother especially."

George snorted. "Not likely," he said. "Mother can't stand the sight of me, haven't you noticed? And Father, well, he always did find me an embarrassment. Nothing I do is good enough for him. Don't you see? This is my one chance to prove myself. I will not go home empty-handed."

This was not going well. Katherine needed time to think. She turned Nugget around. "Shall we head back toward the pack train?" she asked. "You said you needed ammunition."

They walked their horses beside one another in silence, struggling with their own thoughts. Katherine had come so far, she refused to go home empty-handed. Empty-handed, she thought, exactly the words George had used. And then she recalled the other things George had said. *Mother can't stand the sight of me. Father finds me an embarrassment.*

"You're wrong, you know," she said. "I can't imagine why you would think Mother can't stand the sight of you. Even before you left she was always complaining because you were never home. And now — well, she misses you like anything."

George grunted and she glanced over at him. There was something about his grunting that Katherine did not quite understand. It seemed to involve some sort of communication, but to her it was no more than that, simply a grunt, as if he could think of nothing to say but was not content to remain silent.

"It's true. She would give anything to have you back."

George didn't answer. He stared straight ahead.

The grunt was followed by stony silence. Katherine began to realize what it meant. He did not want to talk about it. Well, he was going to have to, sooner or later. She opened her mouth.

"We're almost back," said George. "What did you say your name was?"

"Albert."

"Hmm."


"I see you found him," said the young man in the lead of the pack train. He turned to George. "Sorry to hear about your father."

George grunted.

"It's too bad you have to leave."

"Leave?" asked George.

"Well," the young man glanced toward Katherine, "your kid brother here said — "

"I came back to get more ammunition. We ran out."

George continued on. Katherine followed close behind.

"What are you going to do?" she asked. "Do you think you'll get to the Cariboo, get rich in a couple of weeks, turn around, and come back?"

George ignored her.

"It doesn't work that way, George. The ground up north will soon be frozen, you won't be able to dig. You'll be sitting around starving and freezing in a tiny little log cabin and I'll be at home with an invalid father, a lonely mother, a cellar full of potatoes, and a dead cow."

George stopped his horse and waited for her to catch up. "A dead cow?".

"Of course. Where do you think we'll store the hay for winter? The root cellar? She'll starve to death. And not only that — it's just not fair!"

"What isn't?"

"That you get to go off on an adventure and I have to stay home and eat potatoes."

"Isn't that better than freezing and starving in a little log cabin?"

"No," said Katherine, "I don't think so. In fact, I think I would prefer that. If you won't come home, I'm coming with you."

"Oh, for Pete's sake," said George. He stopped beside a mule and reached over to remove a package from its back. "I've got to take this to the hunting party."

"I'll come with you."

George shook his head. "No. I've got to hurry. You'll never keep up."

"Care to bet on that?"

George laughed. "Don't be ridiculous. You're a girl."

That's all he said. Not that Duke was a faster horse. Not that he, George, was a more experienced rider. Simply that she was a girl.

"I can not only keep up to you," she said, holding back the raw anger from her voice, "I can beat you. And what's more, I'll bet on it. If I lose I'll go home, empty-handed, without another word. If I win, you'll come with me and you won't complain, not once. Agreed?" She held out her hand.

George threw back his head and laughed.

"Agreed?" she insisted, still offering her hand. "It's the only way to get rid of me."

George stopped laughing. "Since you put it that way. Agreed."

They shook hands solemnly.

George stashed the package of ammunition in a saddlebag. "Let's go!" he said and, before Katherine had even turned Nugget around, he kicked Duke on the sides, and took off at a canter.

"Wait!" called Katherine. "That's not fair!" But there was

no stopping George. She swung her horse around. "Come on, Nugget, we can do it!"

She kept Nugget a good length behind Duke. There was no room to pass. The mules became agitated at hearing the horses coming so quickly up behind them. Some stepped sideways in an attempt to get off the trail, others turned their heads nervously, and still others stopped in their tracks. The packers shot them angry looks and shouted as they passed.

"What's the matter with you?"

"Slow down!"

"If I get my hands on you . . . "

Neither George nor Katherine paid them any heed. As soon as they had passed the leading horse, George urged Duke into a gallop.

"Come on, Nugget, you can take him," Katherine called. Nugget needed no further encouragement. She lengthened her stride into an easy gallop and Katherine leaned forward in the saddle.

Katherine realized she was at a disadvantage. She did not know where George was meeting the hunting party, so she had no clear idea of how far they had to go. She needed to stay behind George until the last, until she could see the others, then she would make her move. She only hoped there would be room enough to pass.

Nugget's long legs stretched out, her smooth muscles moved in perfect unison. They had no trouble keeping up to George, and Katherine was glad of yesterday's rain because it meant she and Nugget were not eating dust. They came quickly to the place where Katherine had met George, and raced over the crest of the hill. Soon after, George cut off the trail to the left, setting out over the barren hillside.

Without even working hard, Nugget drew alongside Duke. George glanced over and his jaw dropped open. Katherine threw back her head and laughed. They were evenly matched. Both horses were young, powerful animals in the prime of their lives and in excellent condition. They surged up the gradual slope, necks outstretched, each horse eager to be in the lead. Nugget had the lighter load and could have moved ahead, but Katherine held her back. She could not afford to take a wrong turn. She searched the rolling horizon for some sign of the hunting party.

Down the hill they galloped and up the next. Nugget was beginning to tire. She had been worked hard in the last few days. Duke, on the other hand, had for the most part been travelling at the pace of the heavily loaded mules in the train. Then she heard Duke's heavy breathing. Perhaps, after all, he was out of condition.

As they reached the crest of the next hill, Katherine could hear her horse fighting for breath, could feel her struggle not to lose ground. If they did not see the hunting party very soon all would be lost. She would be forced to rein Nugget in.

They flew over the top of the hill and she saw, not more than two hundred yards away, a small group of men and horses on a flat stretch of ground. "We're almost there," she called to Nugget, leaning farther forward, urging her on with a flick of the rein.

Nugget pulled ahead with such easy grace that Katherine laughed aloud. Once more she lengthened her stride, her neck stretched out. Nothing could stop her now. Duke's hooves thundered behind them. George yelled angrily at Duke to run faster but the horse was breathing with loud, painful gasps.

Nugget streaked toward the men, her mane flying in Katherine's face as she bent low over the horse's neck. The ground passed in a brown blur. She could see their faces now, their eyes wide as they stared at the two horses bearing down upon them. Nugget reached the men and passed them, with Duke more than a length behind.

"We did it!" Katherine shouted, pulling gently on the reins. "Good girl!" They slowed through a canter to a trot.

She turned the horse's head and brought her back slowly to the cluster of men and horses, who still watched in disbelief. George and Duke had veered off in another direction and were heading back now, trotting across the open land.

"Hello," she said as she came up to the men. "I'm Albert, George's brother. He said you wanted the ammunition in a hurry."

"Not in such an all-fired hurry you had to scare off every animal in five miles!" said a tall, heavy-set man with one, thick eyebrow growing right across his forehead. "Ammunition's not much use now!"

"Where the blazes did you come from anyhow?" asked the other, a thin, wiry man with the longest, narrowest nose Katherine had ever seen.

"Sorry," said Katherine, in answer to Eyebrow as she brought Nugget to a stop. "But I had to beat George or he would refuse to come with me." She turned to Long Nose. "I came from our farm near Hope to tell him he's needed at home. Our father's been badly injured."

George reined Duke in beside her. His face was an angry mask.

"Yer little brother here sure knows how to handle a horse," said Long Nose. "Imagine, a little feller like that beatin' the fastest horse and rider in the pack train."

George said nothing. Not even a grunt.

"May as well hand over the ammunition, son," said Long Nose. "So's you can be on yer way."

George's head jerked up. "What?"

Eyebrow narrowed his eyes. "Yer kid brother here tells us yer needed at home 'cause yer Daddy's been hurt. Can't imagine why you gotta settle it with a race but you sure did lose that one!" he chuckled.

"You'll want to get a good start," said Long Nose. "So's you can go a long ways before night."

"What about my supplies?" asked George gloomily.

"Take the food you need," said Long Nose. "The rest'll be waitin' for you at Barkerville when you show up."

"See that it is," said George with an air of misplaced authority that caused the two men to look at each other and shake their heads sadly. "I'll be there in the spring."

They made good time that first day, returning south. Several times Katherine tried to speak to her brother but he refused to answer. At last she stopped trying. Mile after mile they travelled in silence. George insisted on being in the lead which was fine with Katherine because that way she could keep an eye on him. She had visions of him sneaking off to rejoin the pack train when she was not looking.

Now that her mission was almost accomplished she should have been happy. Instead, she felt empty inside, as if she had done something terribly wrong and did not know how to make it better.

"I'm sorry," she said that night as they sat by a camp-fire eating beans and bacon and drinking coffee.

George grunted.

Suddenly Katherine could take no more of it. "Why do you do that?" she demanded. "Why can't you talk to me like a normal human being? You just hang around feeling sorry for yourself as if you're the only person in the world who didn't get to do what he wanted. I used to think that underneath your mean, selfish, lazy exterior there was really a nice person lurking. I used to think that deep down you really did care about your family, but you don't, do you? You just care about yourself. And none of us is good enough for you. Well, if that's the way you plan to be when we get home, if you're just going to sit around and sulk and tell me I'm do-ing everything wrong, if you're not going to help out— then you may as well leave in the morning. I release you from our bet. Go, and get rich or starve to death. Just see if I care!"

George stared at her over the fire. The warm light and

dark shadows played across his face and made him look frightening. He opened his mouth and shut it again. He tossed the dregs of his coffee into the fire, causing it to spit and sizzle. A hiss of smoke shot into the night air. "Are you quite finished?" he asked.

Katherine grunted. If she were going to dress like a boy she may as well act like one. Actually, now that she had tried it, the grunt felt pretty good. She didn't have to make any sort of decision. She avoided saying yes or no. Which left George to decide for himself what she really meant.

"Good. In that case I'm going to sleep." He lay down on his back.

Katherine stared at her brother. He understood a grunt in a way that he never seemed to understand real words. He did not move, but she was certain he was awake, gazing up at the night sky. She wondered what he was thinking. She wondered if he actually thought in words or merely in a series of grunts.

At last, for warmth, she curled up in her blanket and watched the orange flames wriggle under a chunk of log then writhe upward to be swallowed by the night. Beyond the fire she could just make out a dark lump that was George. He was still not asleep, Katherine could tell by his quick, uneasy breathing. She was afraid to fall asleep now herself, afraid that if she did, her brother might not be there in the morning.

# Chapter 18

The glowing embers shrank, became dull. One by one they faded out. Katherine, curled up in a tight ball with her fists clenched fiercely against her chest, watched the few that remained. In her mind she kept going over every little thing George had ever done to hurt her, every cruel word, every disdainful look, every time he had ignored her and made her feel she did not belong.

Once in a while something good would sneak in and she would try to push it away. Like the time she was barely five years old and playing in a park near their home in England. While their nurse chatted with other nurses, forgetting to watch the children, a group of boys started picking on Katherine, pulling at her dress and hair, and calling her the "ugly stepsister." It was George who came to her rescue. He swooped down and chased the little boys away, threatening to give them a beating if they ever came near his sister again. Then he sat beside her on the grass, dried her tears, told her she was not a stepsister and was certainly not ugly — just different. She resembled Father, while Susan and he looked more like their mother.

Another day, about three years ago, Katherine came running through the entrance hall in their grandmother's house. She swung around a corner on the polished wood floor, skidded, and bumped smack into a small table. She tried to catch the vase but it toppled off the far side and shattered into a thousand pieces. Father stormed into the hall and let go a torrent of words that even now were painful to recall. To her amazement, George stepped between them and insisted it was all his fault, because he had been chasing Katherine. This was not true, yet he said it anyway, and Father's rage turned on him. Katherine had never asked him why he did that. She had never even thanked him.

Now she shifted uncomfortably on the hard ground, and unclenched her fists. She went over the harsh words she had spoken to George this evening and began to feel sorry. She should never have told him she did not care about him. What if he left in the night? What if something happened to him and she never saw him again? She must tell him she was sorry, that she had not meant it. She must thank him for the things he had done. She licked her lips and opened her mouth, but the words would not come. They stuck in her throat as if something were blocking them.

She closed her eyes. The small embers of the fire imprinted themselves on her eyelids. They began to move, slowly at first and then more quickly, making circles, leaving bright trails behind them. They slowed again, but now they were pieces of gold, nuggets of all sizes lying in a bed of sand, all of them shaped like roses. She bent to pick one up. Someone was behind her, watching. Katherine swung around. It was Susan, looking very tired.

"George doesn't want to come home," Katherine told her. "I've come all this way for nothing. I should have known better than to think George would want to help us."

"Don't you understand?" Susan asked quietly. "Can't you see that George is afraid?"

"Huh! What on earth has he got to be afraid of? He simply doesn't want to be bothered with us. You were the only one he cared about."

"Nevertheless, he is afraid," Susan repeated.

"Of what?" Katherine demanded.

Susan did not answer.

"Tell me! I don't understand!"

"Who are you talking to?" George's voice.

Katherine opened her eyes. She looked up at the stars, high above the treetops, and shivered under her thin blanket.

"Who are you talking to?" George repeated.

"No one," said Katherine. "I must have been dreaming. Susan was there. She says you are afraid."

"Me? Afraid?"

"That's what she said. But I don't understand. Are you afraid of going home?"

George did not answer, not even a grunt.

"Are you?"

"Not afraid, exactly." He paused, cleared his throat. "It's just — I know what everyone thinks. They hate me for what I did. Especially you."

Katherine let this sink in, then asked quietly, "What did you do?"

George seemed to find talk easier when he could not be seen. As if a voice out of the darkness could not be so easily hurt. "Don't you think I can see it? Every time you look at me you see Susan and you wish I had died instead of her. Don't you think I know how close you and Susan were? You hate the sight of me because you know I'm the one person who could have helped her."

Katherine could not believe what she was hearing. George blamed himself? She had always thought —

"Why you?" she asked, her words rising into the dark night. "I'm the one she waited on when I was seasick, when she was so tired. If I hadn't been sick — "

"But you were. And I wasn't. I should have helped her instead of always standing around, complaining about being bored."

"Susan," Katherine whispered, "did you hear that? I can't believe it. They all think it's their fault when all the time it was me. I'm the real guilty one. But — I didn't know it would be this way! Honest I didn't!"

"Are you talking to yourself again?" asked George.

"Yes," said Katherine, "maybe I am. George, it wasn't your fault Susan died. No one blames you, me least of all. You see, it was all my fault. I always wanted to do something — anything — better than Susan, and I wanted it by the time I was fourteen. On my birthday I got my wish. There was nothing I could do better than her as long as she was alive. The only thing I could possibly do better is — to live!"

There was a short pause, then "You're crazy!" George's voice exploded, like a burst of sparks from the fire.

Katherine stared up at the sky. The stars began to blur and she blinked away tears. There was a lump in her throat. Suddenly she realized George was sitting beside her. His hand lightly touched her shoulder, then moved away. She sat up.

"You're wrong, you know," George said quietly. "Susan didn't die because of your silly wish. Maybe she didn't even die because of me. Maybe she would have died anyway. Who knows? I only know I'd give anything to make her alive again."

"Yes," said Katherine. Her throat had such a great lump in it she could scarcely breathe. "Maybe," she whispered, "for Susan's sake, we should try being nice to each other."

George grunted. He thought for a minute. "All right," he said finally, "I think I could manage that." He gently patted her shoulder and went back to his side of the fire where, Katherine could tell by the scuffling sounds, he lay down again. "You know something?" he asked.

"What?"

"Susan would be proud of us."

Katherine curled up again, her fist pressed hard against

her lips. Before long she heard soft snoring from across the dead fire. She felt a small, hard lump against her hip and turned on her back to pull the gold rose nugget out of her pocket. She clutched it against her chest.

"Thank you, Susan," she whispered. "Thank you for putting up with us for so long. And now we are ready to manage on our own. I'm sure of it. I promise not to call you back. I promise not to trouble you again. But I hope it won't bother you too much if I just keep you in my heart. Just a part of you. Just your memory."

She opened her eyes and held the nugget up between her fingers, trying to see its shape under the pale light of the moon. "I'll keep the golden rose, too," she said. "I never want to get rid of it now. I've decided it doesn't bring good luck or bad either, it's only a piece of gold. But, if I ever have children, I'll show it to them and tell them about you. They'll be proud to have an aunt like you."

She turned onto her side and closed her eyes, holding the nugget tightly in her closed fist.

When Katherine next opened her eyes the sun was high in the sky. There was a cheerful fire burning and the smell of strong coffee wafted toward her from the blackened pot.

She sat up, slid the nugget into its bag in her pocket, and stretched her arms above her head. She couldn't remember ever sleeping so soundly or awaking so refreshed. Suddenly she froze. George was not on the far side of the fire. She looked around. He was nowhere in sight. She leaped to her feet.

"It's about time you woke up!" George called and Katherine almost gasped with relief. He was walking back from the river, his hair dripping wet and plastered down against his head. "We've wasted half the morning because of you!" He grinned and dropped down beside the fire to pour himself some of the thick, black coffee he had made.

"Oh, quit your complaining," said Katherine. "You should have started ahead of me. That way, I wouldn't have to keep waiting for you to catch up."

"We'll see about that." George held the pot toward her. "Want some coffee?"

"Is that what you call it? It looks more like mud from the bottom of a duck pond."

He shrugged and leaned forward to replace the pot beside the fire.

"But I'll have some anyway," she said, "just to keep you happy."

George shook his head and grunted as he poured the coffee.

# Dayle Campbell Gaetz

Dayle Gaetz first dipped her paddle into the waters of B.C. history when she was playing in the ocean around Victoria with her childhood friends. "Down on the beach, below the steep cliffs, it was possible," Dayle says, "to imagine that the city above us did not yet exist." The logs were their canoes and they themselves were explorers seeing the shoreline for the first time. Dayle has now taken her imaginative forays into the past into her most recent novel for young readers.

Dayle Gaetz lives on Salt Spring Island with her husband, Gary. When she is not reading or writing, or playing with her grandchildren, Dayle is hiking around Mount Robson or Cowichan Lake or boating in the beautiful ocean waters of Desolation Sound. She is also an avid museum visitor.

Also by Dayle Campbell Gaetz

---

# *A Sea Lion Called Salena*

Kristie is a lonely 9-year-old who discovers a wounded sea lion pup hiding under a wharf near her home. She tries to befriend and help Salena, but soon realizes that the pup needs more care than she can give. When Salena is also threatened by local fishers, Kristie joins forces with new friends to help Salena survive.

For ages 8-11. ISBN 0-88865-069-8. $8.95

Other children's fiction from Pacific Educational Press

Co
A                                                                    mining
co                                                              -88865-
09

| | DATE DUE | |
|---|---|---|
| Co | | |
| Th | | | 0. ISBN |
| 0-8 | | | |
| | | | |
| An | | | |
| A | | | era. For |
| rea | | | |
| | | | |
| Jan | | | |
| A | | | C. coast |
| wit | | | ced by |
| the | | | any it. |
| For | | | ok and |
| vid | | | |

$11.00

Al
A                                                                    people
wl                                                              . $9.95

FIC   Gaetz, Dayle Campbell
GAE      The golden rose
pbk.

Fo                                                                   titles,
co                                                              ation,
Ur                                                              1Z4,
tel